Clara Roscom

Anatiposi

Anonymous

Clara Roscom

Reprint of the original.

1st Edition 2023 | ISBN: 978-3-38210-636-2

Anatiposi Verlag is an imprint of Outlook Verlagsgesellschaft mbH.

Verlag (Publisher): Outlook Verlag GmbH, Zeilweg 44, 60439 Frankfurt, Deutschland
Vertretungsberechtigt (Authorized to represent): E. Roepke, Zeilweg 44, 60439 Frankfurt, Deutschland
Druck (Print): Books on Demand GmbH, In de Tarpen 42, 22848 Norderstedt, Deutschland

Clara Roscom;

OR,

THE PATH OF DUTY.

BY THE AUTHOR OF ERNEST HARWOOD.

Toronto:

PRINTED BY HUNTER, ROSE AND COMPANY.

MDCCCLXXI.

CONTENTS.

CHAPTER I.

A SUDDEN BEREAVEMENT.

"AWAKE, my dear child, awake!" These were the words I heard. I started up, gazing in a bewildered manner into the face of my mother, who had, with some difficulty, succeeded in arousing me from the sweet, healthful sleep of childhood. My mother drew nigh to me and whispered, "My dear Clara, your papa is dying." With a frightened cry, I threw my arms around her neck, and begged her to tell me what had happened. I was unable to comprehend the meaning of her words. Since my earliest recollection, my father had never experienced a day's illness, and so the reader may be able to form some idea of the shock occasioned by her words—uttered, as they were, at the hour of midnight. When my mother had succeeded in soothing me, in some degree, to calmness, she informed me, in a voice choked with sobs, which, for my sake, she tried to suppress, that my father had, two hours since, been stricken with apoplexy, in so severe a form that his life was despaired of. She further informed me that his attending physician thought he would not live to see the light of another morning. Well do I remember the nervous terror with which I clung to my mother as we entered my father's apartment, and the icy chill which diffused itself over my body, as I gazed upon the fearfully changed features of my father. I had never before seen death in any form. I believe the first view of death is more or less terrible to every child; it certainly was terrible for me to first view death imprinted upon the countenance of a fond father. I have ever since thought that my father recognized me when my mother led me to his bed-side; but power of utterance was gone. It was a fearful trial to me, who had seen but ten years of life. After the first shock, a strange calm took possession of me. Though many years have passed since that period, I remember, as though it were but of yesterday, how I sat during those long hours, scarcely for an instant removing my eyes from my father's face, but shed not a tear; for, after the first burst of grief, tears refused to come to my relief. Just as the day began to dawn I heard the physician say, in a whisper, to a kind neighbor who stood by, I think he is going. At that moment my father opened his eyes, and, looking upward with a pleasant smile, expired without a struggle. I could never clearly remember how I passed the intervening days between my father's death and burial. I have an indistinct recollection of the hushed voices and soft footsteps of friends and neighbors, who kindly came to aid in performing the last offices of love and friendship to the remains of my departed father. I also remember being led by my almost heart-broken mother into the darkened room, where lay the lifeless body of my father, now prepared for the grave; but I have a more vivid recollection of standing with my mother beside an open grave, and hearing our pastor, in a solemn voice, utter the words, "Earth to earth—ashes to ashes—dust to dust." Oh! the falling of that first earth upon my father's coffin, shall I ever forget the sound? Child as I was, it seemed to me that my heart would break; but tears, the first I had shed since my father's death, came to my relief. Those blessed tears. I may well call them blessed, since the physician afterwards told my mother that they saved either my reason or my life. Kind friends besought my mother and me to allow ourselves to be conveyed home, and not await the filling up of the grave. But no. We could not leave the spot till the last earth was thrown upon the grave, and a mound covered with grassy sods was to be seen, where a little before was only a mournful cavity. Then indeed we felt that he was gone, and that we must return to our desolate home

—the home which ever before his presence had filled with joy and gladness.

I must pass over, with a few words only, the first year of our bereavement, as even now I shudder to recall the feeling of loneliness and desolation which took possession of us, when we found ourselves left alone in the home where everything reminded us so strongly of the departed one. There was a small apartment adjoining our usual sitting-room which my father was won't to call his study, and, being fond of books, he used there to pass much of his leisure time. It was quite a long time after his death before my mother could enter that apartment. She said to me one day, "will you go with me Clara to your father's study?" I replied, "can you go *there*, Mamma?" "Yes, dear," said my mother, and led the way to the door. No one had entered that room since my father left it on the last night of his life, the door having been locked on the day succeeding his death. As my mother softly turned the key and opened the door, it seemed almost that we stood in my father's presence, so vividly did the surroundings of that room recall him to our minds. There stood his table and chair, his writing desk stood upon the table, and several books and papers were scattered carelessly upon the table. The last book he had been reading lay open as he had left it; it was a volume of Whitfield's sermons; it was a book which my father valued highly, and it is now a cherished keep-sake of my own. My mother seemed quite overcome with grief. I know she had striven daily to conceal her grief when in my presence, for she knew how I grieved for my father; and she was aware that her tears would only add to my sorrow, so for my sake it was that she forced herself to appear calm—almost cheerful; but upon this occasion her grief was not to be checked. She bowed her head upon the table, while convulsive sobs shook her frame. I tried, in my childish way, to comfort her. I had never seen her so much moved since my father's death. When she became more composed, she rose, and I assisted her in dusting and arranging the furniture of the room; and after this first visit to the room, we no longer avoided entering it. Since quite a young man, my father had been employed as book-keeper in a large mercantile house in the city of Philadelphia, where we resided. As he had ever proved trustworthy and faithful to the interests of his employers, they had seen fit, upon his marriage, to give him an increase of salary, which enabled him to purchase a small, but neat and convenient, dwelling in a respectable street in Philadelphia, where we had lived in the enjoyment of all the comforts, and with many of the luxuries of life, to the time of the sad event which left me fatherless and my mother a widow. I had never, as yet, attended any school. My mother had been my only teacher, and as her own education had been thorough, she was amply qualified for the task.

CHAPTER II.

SUCCESS AT SCHOOL.

ABOUT a year after my father's death, my mother decided upon sending me to school, as she thought I was becoming too sedate and serious for a child only eleven years of age. I had never been very familiar with the neighbouring children of my own age, and after the death of my father I cared still less for their companionship. My chief enjoyment was in the society of my mother, and as we kept no servant, I found many ways of making myself useful to her; and every afternoon she devoted two or three hours to my lessons and needlework. Thus passed away the first year after our great sorrow, when, as I have already said, my mother decided upon sending me to school. It seemed to me, at the time, quite a formidable undertaking—this going to school. I had never been separated from my mother, and the five hours to be spent daily in the schoolroom seemed to my childish mind a very long time. I had ever been shy and diffident in the presence of strangers, and the idea of entering a large school, a stranger to both teacher and pupils, was very unpleasant to me. But when I found it to be my mother's wish that I should go, I endeavoured to overcome my reluctance, and assisted my mother in her preparations for entering me as a pupil at the beginning of the ensuing term.

It was with a feeling of timidity that I accompanied my mother through several streets to the school taught by Miss Edmonds. My mother accompanied me to relieve me from any awkwardness I might feel in presenting myself for admission. It was a select school for girls. As my education had thus far been entirely conducted by my mother, I had, of course, never been subjected to the rules of a school-room; and I must confess that I had formed an idea of school teachers in general that was not at all flattering. I fancied them all to be old, sour and cross—a mere walking bundle of rules and regulations, and I was quite unprepared to see the sweet looking young lady who answered to my mother's summons at the door. Surely, thought I, this young lady cannot be Miss Edmonds; and when my mother enquired if such were her name and she replied in the affirmative, I thought going to school might not be so bad after all. After giving Miss Edmonds my name and age, my mother held some conversation with her regarding my studies, and left me with an encouraging smile. I felt all my timidity return when I thought of entering the school-room with Miss Edmonds, but her kind and friendly manner reassured me. The school consisted of about thirty girls, many of them older than myself. I had feared that my attainments would be inferior to those of the youngest of the pupils, and I was equally pleased and surprised when Miss Edmonds, after a long and careful examination in regard to my acquirements, placed me in one of the higher classes. There was to me an irresistable attraction in the countenance and manner of my teacher; and, from the first moment I saw her, I loved her. Although her home is now far distant from mine, and we have not met for many years, I love her as dearly now as when she took me by the hand when a child of eleven years. She conducted her school in a very systematic and orderly manner, and was very particular to require perfect recitations from her pupils; but, as I possessed a retentive memory, I found my tasks much lighter than did many of my classmates.

When I had been about a year at school, Miss Edmonds offered a prize, in the class to which I belonged, to the young lady who should write the most able composition, upon a given subject. The prize was to be a small gold pencil-case, and was to be awarded at the close of the summer term. The closing day at length came; there was much suppressed excitement when we were called to order that morning. As we expected no visitors till the afternoon, we spent the morning mostly in reviewing our various studies. By two o'clock our schoolroom was crowded. We first passed a very searching examination in the different studies we had pursued during the past year. I believe we passed our examination in a manner creditable both to our teacher and to ourselves.

The reading of our compositions was reserved, as the closing exercise. The compositions, with the name of the writer, were read by Miss Edmonds. Each person present was at liberty to write down each name as it was read by our teacher, annexing to it the numbers one, two or three, according to their opinion of the merits of the composition, each desk being furnished with paper, pens and ink for the purpose. When the compositions had all been read, the slips of paper were collected and handed to our pastor, who was to read aloud the fortunate name with the greatest number of ones annexed. What then was my amazement and that of all present when our pastor, after carefully examining the papers, rose and said,—"Miss Clara Roscom will please come forward, and receive from the hands of Miss Edmonds the reward of so much merit." I remember I felt a nervous dread of crossing the large school-room alone, when I knew every eye would be directed to me. Composing myself by a strong effort, I rose and walked up to the raised platform, where at her desk sat Miss Edmonds, with our pastor and several other friends. As I bowed low in acknowledgment of the gift, Miss Edmonds, with a few kind words, dismissed me to my seat, I heard many flattering remarks among our assembled friends; but the proudest moment of all, to me, was when I gained my mother's side and she said to me in a low voice, "My dear Clara, this seems to me a token that you will prove a blessing to your poor widowed mother."

Miss Edmonds often remarked that I made wonderful progress in my studies, and these commendations, coming from my teacher, incited me to still greater diligence. I take no credit to myself for superior talent, but I certainly did my best, for, be it remembered, I was studying to please my dear mother, who often said to me, "You must, my dear Clara, make the best of your opportunities for improvement, as the time may come when your education may be your only means of support." My mother often regretted that we did not own a piano, for she was very anxious that I should study music;

but our means did not justify the purchase of an instrument, and she thought that lessons without the necessary practice would be useless. The parents of Miss Edmonds resided in the city. They had once been wealthy, but owing to those reverses to which all are liable they had become reduced in circumstances, so much so that Miss Edmonds gladly turned to account the superior education she had received in their prosperous days, and she had for some time been a teacher when I became a member of her school. My mother happened to mention to Miss Edmonds one day her regret that I was unable to take music-lessons, for want of opportunity for the needful practice, when she informed my mother that she still retained her piano out of the wreck of their former affluence, and that, if she wished me to take lessons, I was at liberty to practice daily upon it. My mother accepted for me the kind offer, and I at once began taking lessons. I remained four years under the instruction of Miss Edmonds, with much profit to myself. At the end of this time, Mr. Edmonds removed with his family to the city of New York, having, through the influence of friends, obtained the situation of cashier in one of the banks in that city. It was a severe trial for Miss Edmonds to resign the school where she was so much beloved by her pupils; but she thought it her duty to accompany her parents to their new home.

CHAPTER III.

CLARA AT MRS. WENTWORTH'S BOARDING SCHOOL.

AS it was my mother's intention to give me a thoroughly good education, she began, after the departure of Miss Edmonds, to consider the propriety of sending me to a noted seminary for young ladies, about two hundred miles from Philadelphia, as she learned from various sources of the excellence of the institution. There was but one difficulty in the way, and that was the money needful for defraying my expenses. At my father's death, he left us the owners of the house we occupied, and a sum of money, though not a large one, in the savings' bank. Up to the time of which I speak, we had only drawn the annual interest of our money, while the principal remained untouched, my mother having obtained needle-work to eke out our small income; but, in order that I should finish my education according to the wishes of my mother, as well as my own, a portion of the principal must be withdrawn. After some reflection upon the subject, my mother decided that a good education might prove of more value to me than money, so a portion of the money was drawn, and we began the preparations for my departure from home. It was the high reputation which the school sustained that influenced my mother in her decision to send me so far from home. There was a lady residing in the near vicinity of the school who had been a loved school-mate of my mother in their youthful days. My mother wrote to her upon the subject and received a very friendly reply, informing her that, owing to their own early friendship, she would be most happy to fill a mother's place to me, so long as I should wish to remain at school. I should have been much elated at the proposed journey had it not been for the thought of leaving my mother, who had ever been my confidant and adviser. My mother also felt keenly the coming departure, although she strove to conceal her feelings as much as possible. I strongly objected to leaving her alone, but we had as yet been unable to devise any plan to avoid so doing. My mother would have rented a portion of our dwelling, but it was not adapted for the convenience of two families, neither could she endure the disquiet of keeping boarders.

"Clara," said my mother, one day, as we sat at work, "I think I will send for Aunt Patience to come and stay with me during your absence."

She laughed outright at the look of dismay with which I regarded her, occasioned by the recollection which I retained of a visit she paid us when I was eight years of age. She was a maiden lady somewhat advanced in years, possessed of a very kind heart and many excellent qualities; but the name of Patience seemed to me a misapplication in her case, for she certainly possessed but a small quantity of that valuable article. Early in life she had passed through many trials, which might have tended to sour her disposition. I remember that during the visit referred to, my mother had occasion to spend a day from home, leaving me in the care of Aunt Patience. It seemed a very long day to me. Like all children, I was restless and troublesome, and to one unaccustomed to the care of children it was doubtless very annoying. During the day I received a severe box on the ear from Aunt Patience, for saying to her in an outburst of childish anger, when provoked by her continued fault-finding,

"I don't know what makes them call you Aunt Patience, for you scold all the time."

She informed my mother of it upon her return, and she gave me a reproof for allowing myself to speak disrespectfully to my relative; although, while listening to the relation of the difficulty by Aunt Patience, she found it extremely difficult to repress a smile. However, my mother both loved and respected her, and thought she could live very comfortably with her during my absence; indeed my mother thought her quite a desirable companion, for, setting aside her irritability at petty annoyances, she was a woman of good sense, and was well informed upon most subjects, so I gladly joined in the invitation which my mother sent her, to come and make our house her home for an indefinite period. As she lived only a day's journey by railway from Philadelphia, she arrived a week before I left home. She did not like the idea of my mother spending so much money in sending me to school. To all of her remarks upon the subject my mother replied pleasantly, for she was her own aunt, and she would not treat her with disiespect. During the few days I remained at home after her arrival, I formed a much more favorable opinion of Aunt Patience than I had done during her visit in the days of my childhood; and when I observed how kind she was to my mother I found it easy to love her.

I felt very sad the morning I bade adieu to my mother and Aunt Patience, to go into the world alone. My mother had before given me many kind counsels regarding my future conduct, but now she only said, as she embraced me at parting, "My dear daughter, I trust you will improve your time and talents, and conduct yourself in a manner that will not disappoint your mother." As Aunt Patience bade me good-bye, she said, with a countenance of much solemnity, "You must remember, Clara, all the advice I have given you." Sad as I felt, I could not repress a smile, for during the past week her advices regarding my future conduct had been so numerous, that it would have required a memory more retentive than mine to have remembered them all; but I knew they were intended for my good, and I readily promised to try and observe them. I wish not to weary the reader by giving a detailed account of my journey. I arrived safely at my destination, and met with a very cordial welcome at the house of Mrs. Armitage, my mother's friend; and two days later I became a member of the celebrated school for young ladies, taught at that time by Mrs. Wentworth, aided by competent assistants.

Mrs. Wentworth was a widow lady, of superior education and noble mind. I spent four happy years in this institution, having visited my mother but once during the time. It was very pleasant for me to find myself once more at home, with the opportunity for rest and relaxation, after four years' application to books. During my absence my mother and Aunt Patience had lived very quietly, they saw but little company, and were much occupied with their needles as a means of support. During the first three years of my absence my mother enjoyed good health, but during my last year at school, she was visited by a long and painful illness, through which she was attended, with the utmost kindness and attention, by her aunt; my mother being unwilling to recall me from school, if it were possible to avoid it; and she had been obliged, on account of her illness, to withdraw most of the sum remaining in the savings' bank. On my return home I found her enjoying a tolerable degree of health, but I feared that such close application to her needle had been too much for one whose constitution was naturally delicate. She seemed like one weary both in mind and body. After my arrival, however, she seemed to regain her usual cheerfulness, and in a short time seemed quite herself again. It was now that I felt it to be my duty to turn the education which my mother had been at so much pains to give me to account by teaching, in order to assist her, and also to obtain a support for myself. We had decided to offer Aunt Patience a home for the remainder of her life, indeed I felt that I owed her a debt of gratitude for her past kindness to my mother. We therefore told her that so long as we possessed a home, we would gladly share it with her, provided she felt contented to remain with us. She at first demurred a little, as she was aware that our means were limited; but when my mother told her that she would not know what to do without her, it seemed to set her mind at rest, and she gladly assented to our proposal, and it was settled that for the future her home was to be with us.

I had as yet settled upon no definite plan in regard to teaching. My mother wished me to apply for the situation of governess in a family, as she thought that position would command a higher salary, and would prove less laborious than a situation in a school. About this time we noticed in a daily paper an advertisement for a governess, wanted in the family of a Mr. Leighton, residing in the suburbs of the city; the salary offered was liberal, and I thought, with my mother, that I had best apply for the situation.

CHAPTER IV.

GOVERNESS IN MR. LEIGHTON'S FAMILY.

IT was with a feeling of trepidation, such as I never before experienced, that I ascended the steps of the splendid residence of Mr. Leighton. When I found myself at the door my courage well nigh failed me, but without giving myself much time for reflection, I rang the door bell. After some little delay the door was opened by a domestic, of whom I enquired if I could see Mrs. Leighton. The servant replied that she did not know, but that she would see if her mistress was disengaged. "What name?" enquired the servant, "Miss Roscom," I replied. The servant ushered me into the parlor, and left the room. Being left alone, I amused myself by taking a survey of the apartment. It was evident that I had entered the abode of luxury and wealth. The sofas and chairs were covered with rich velvet, while satin curtains draped the windows. An elegant and costly piano occupied one corner of the room; the walls were adorned by costly pictures, and on the marble centre-table were many books in elegant bindings; and rare and exquisite ornaments were scattered with lavish profusion. Upon the entrance of a tall, and, as I thought at the time, rather haughty-looking, lady, I rose, bowed and continued standing, as she said,—

"My servant informs me your name is Miss Roscom."

I replied in the affirmative, and added, "I have the pleasure, I presume, of addressing Mrs. Leighton?"

The lady acknowledged her claim to that name, and I continued,—"Seeing your advertisement for a governess, I have made bold to apply for the situation."

The lady bent upon me a searching look, as she replied,—

"Pray be seated Miss, and we will converse upon the matter."

I gladly obeyed her request that I should be seated, for I felt nervous and agitated. After a moment's silence she addressed me, saying,—

"You look rather young for the responsible duties of a governess."

I replied that I was not yet nineteen years of age, that I had not as yet been engaged in teaching, having only myself left school three months since,—but that I found it necessary that I should do something for my own support and that of my widowed mother,

—and that I would gladly do my utmost to give satisfaction, could I obtain a situation.

Mrs. Leighton, after a moment's thought, said,—"Although you are young for the position, your countenance pleases me, and I feel inclined to give you a trial."

She then informed me that my pupils would consist of two girls, the eldest twelve, the other ten years of age, also a little boy of seven. She added,

"I had almost forgotten to enquire if you have brought any references?"

Whereupon I handed her the certificate of qualifications given me by Mrs. Wentworth when I left school. She looked pleased as she replied,

"Your being for four years a member of Mrs. Wentworth's school is in itself a recommendation."

I also handed her the names of several ladies well known in the city, telling her she was at liberty to make any enquiries of them she might think proper. She replied that she felt almost certain she would engage me, but that she would send me a decided answer in the course of two or three days. I thanked her, and, bidding a good morning, set out on my return home, much elated with the success of this my first application.

The salary offered by Mrs. Leighton was a weighty consideration to me, and although aware that my duties would often prove unpleasant and irksome, I felt that I could endure much, with the consciousness that I was assisting my dear mother.

My mother advised me not to be too sanguine, as I might not obtain the situation; but, on the third day after my application, my suspense was relieved by receiving a note from Mrs. Leighton, saying that she would gladly engage me, if I still wished for the situation; and she named an early day when she wished me to enter upon my duties. I replied that I gladly accepted the situation, and would be ready to begin duties at the day appointed.

Now that I had accepted of the position, I began to experience many doubts as to my success in the undertaking. I had no knowledge as yet of the dispositions of the children that were to be committed to my care, not having even seen them; but my mother told me I was wrong to allow such thoughts to trouble me, and that the blessing of God would surely rest upon my labors so long as I continued in the path of duty. I therefore cast away all my desponding fears, and hastened the preparations for my departure to the home of the Leightons.

I was kindly received by Mrs. Leighton upon my arrival; and, when we were seated in the parlor, she summoned the children for the purpose of introducing them to me.

"My dears," said she, addressing the children, "this is Miss Roscom, your governess."

Then, turning to me, she introduced them each by name. I must confess that I was not prepossessed in favour of the eldest of the girls. She was very tall for her age; she had a dark complexion, with very black eyes and hair, and had, as it seemed to me, rather a forbidding expression of countenance. She also gave me, as I thought, rather pert replies to the few remarks I addressed to her. There was not the slightest resemblance between her and her younger sister; her name was Georgania. There was something peculiarly attractive in the countenance and manner of Bertha, or Birdie, as she was called by all the family. She was indeed a child formed to attract the admiration and love of all who saw her. Her complexion would have appeared almost too pale but for the rose-tint on either cheek; she had beautiful eyes, of a dark blue, and her soft, brown hair fell in luxuriant curls upon her shoulders. She came forward as her mother called her name, and placed her hand in mine. I thought at the time that I had never before seen so lovely and engaging a child. The little boy, Lewis, was a manly-looking little fellow for his age, although I feared, from his countenance, that he might possess a temper and a will not easy to be controlled. He somewhat resembled his sister Georgania, as his complexion and eyes were dark; but he had a more pleasing expression of countenance. When Mrs. Leighton had dismissed the children from the room, she turned to me, remarking that probably I would like to retire for a time to my own room, she called one of the servants and requested her to show me to my apartment. As I was leaving the parlor she informed me that tea would be ready at half-past six o'clock. The room appropriated to my use was very pleasant, and was also tastefully furnished. At the tea-table I was introduced to Mr. Leighton, whom I had not before seen. I was very much pleased by his manner, which had none of that patronizing condescension with which the rich so often address the poor. I found him a gentleman, in the truest sense of the word.

After tea, Mr. Leighton requested me to favor them with some music. Accordingly I seated myself at the piano and played several pieces, with which he seemed much pleased. He remarked that they were quite at a loss for music since their eldest daughter, Laura, left home for school, as their two youngest daughters had but recently commenced taking lessons. As I rose from the piano, Mrs. Leighton enquired if I sang. I replied that I sometimes sang to oblige my friends. She asked if I would favour them with a song. Resuming my seat, I began the first song which occurred to my mind. It chanced to be that much-admired song, by Foster, called "Willie, we have missed you." When I concluded I was surprised to find Mrs. Leighton in tears. She informed me, by way of apology, that their eldest son's name was Willie, and that he had been absent for some months in England, on account of the death of a wealthy uncle, who had made him his heir. She remarked, further, that he was the life of their dwelling, and they had indeed missed him very much, I said that I was sorry to have given her pain. She replied that the song had afforded her a pleasure, although, said she, "I could not refrain from tears while thinking of my absent Willie."

In order to change the subject, Mr. Leighton remarked that they were fortunate in securing a governess who could both sing and play, as he was very fond of music.

When I left Mrs. Wentworth's school I was called an excellent performer on the piano, for I was very fond of music, and had devoted much time to practice. We also enjoyed some very pleasant conversation during the evening, and the more I saw of Mr. and Mrs. Leighton I felt disposed to like them. When I retired to my own room I kneeled and thanked my Heavenly Father for directing me to a home where I had a prospect of being useful and happy.

It is not my intention to give a detailed account of the events of the next two years; and a few words must suffice for that period of time.

If I had trials of temper to endure from my pupils, —and who ever yet was a governess and had not,— I also enjoyed much pleasure in their society. The eldest of my pupils gave me more trouble than did both the others. Her memory was not retentive; she had also a certain listlessness of manner during lessons which was at times very annoying. But it was a very pleasant task to instruct Birdie; she drank in knowledge eagerly, and possessed an excellent memory. In music she made astonishing progress, for a child of her years; and she was of a most affectionate disposition, which made the duty of imparting knowledge to her doubly pleasant. The progress of little Lewis was equal to that of most boys of his age. I found less trouble with him than I had at the first anticipated. I found him to be a child that would never be controlled by harshness, but he was easily restrained by kindness.

As often as I could do so conveniently I visited my mother and Aunt Patience. Aunt Patience seemed happier than I had ever before seen her. I think the quiet of her home tended to soften her somewhat irritable temper.

CHAPTER V.

WILLIE LEIGHTON'S RETURN FROM ENGLAND.

SOON after I became a resident in the dwelling of Mr. Leighton, they received a letter from Willie, informing them that the estate of his deceased relative could not be finally arranged in less time than a year, perhaps longer; and he thought that instead of returning to Philadelphia he would enter a College in England, and devote the intervening time to study. His parents could not object, knowing it to be for his interest, as he had not, when a boy, taken very kindly to study. A year passed away, and Willie did not return, but they received frequent letters from him. Near the close of the second year he wrote, informing them that he intended leaving England on the tenth of the month following, as the matters pertaining to the property left him were now satisfactorily arranged.

About this time Laura returned home from school, having finished her term of study. Mrs. Leighton intended sending Georgania to the same institution where Laura studied, but she was not to go till the coming autumn. She wished, however, that I should remain with them till Birdie and Lewis should be old enough to send from home. I had been very, *very* kindly treated in the home of Mrs. Leighton, and had become strongly attached to my pupils, especially the two younger of them; and I was glad of the opportunity of remaining near to my mother.

As the time drew near when they looked for the return of Willie, all the family were busy with their preparations for giving him a joyous welcome.

When I observed the eagerness with which they looked forward to his return, I could not at times help feeling a pang of regret that I had neither brother nor sister of my own. Had it not been for my surviving parent, I should have felt entirely alone in the world. Not that I envied the Leightons—far from it—but I could not help sometimes contrasting my position in life with theirs. They being blessed with the love of fond parents, brothers and sisters, along with the possession of abundant wealth, and every comfort which tends to form a happy home; while I was a poor, fatherless girl, obliged to labor for my own support and that of my mother. I could not help thinking how different all might have been had the life of my father been spared. I do not think that I was usually of an unhappy disposition; on the contrary, I was inclined to be hopeful and cheerful; but I believe that, with the best of us, the happiness of others more favored than ourselves will sometimes give rise to a feeling of sadness.

The time soon arrived when, according to the letter they had received from Willie, they might daily expect his arrival. None of the family were able to settle their minds upon any employment, and it was with the greatest difficulty that I could obtain the attention of my pupils during the time appointed for their daily lessons, and, being aware of the cause, I could hardly blame them. Their suspense was at length ended by the arrival of Willie. Never shall I forget the joy which was depicted upon the countenance of little Lewis when he suddenly burst into my room, exclaiming,

"Oh! Miss Roscom, our dear, *dear* brother Willie has come at last! Don't you wish you had a brother Willie too?"

Had he known the pang which his childish remark occasioned me he certainly would never have made it. With much difficulty I kept back my tears and tried to appear as much pleased as the child evidently wished me to be. I had been accustomed, since my residence in the family, to spend my evenings mostly with them in the parlor; but on that evening I remained in my own room, feeling that I should be an intruder upon that family reunion. I took up a book and endeavored to interest myself in its pages. I could distinctly hear the joyous murmur of voices from below, varied by bursts of laughter, not loud, but strikingly mirthful. I soon heard light footsteps ascending the stairs; the next moment Birdie rushed in, exclaiming,

"Mamma says she has been so much occupied that she had almost forgotten you; but she says you must come down at once; you mustn't sit here alone when we are all so happy."

I begged to be excused from going down, saying that they would probably prefer being left to themselves on this first evening of Willie's return.

"Oh!" said she, "Papa and mamma both expect you to go down."

Fearful of giving offence, and after making some slight alterations in my dress, I accompanied Birdie down stairs and entered the parlor.

I believe most persons feel a kind of embarrassment when meeting for the first time one of whom they have long heard much. I was sensible of this feeling when I entered the parlor that evening.

Willie rose as I entered the room, and Mrs. Leighton, coming forward, said,—

"Miss Roscom, allow me to introduce to you my son Willie."

I felt much relieved by this unceremonious introduction. For a time we engaged in general conversation. The manner of Willie was so genial and pleasant that I at once felt at ease in his society. I had often thought that Birdie resembled no other member of the family, but that was before I saw Willie. He had the same complexion, the same cast of countenance, with the same smile, only in a more mature and masculine form.

After an hour spent in social conversation, he said some music would be very welcome to him, it was so long since he had enjoyed that pleasure in their own home. Laura immediately went to the piano, and sang two or three songs which she knew to be favourites of his. Willie invited me to play, but I begged him to excuse me for the time being, as he had three sisters present, who all played more or less.

After his sisters had each in their turn favoured him with some music, he rose, and taking the vacant seat at the piano, asked if we would not like to hear an English song. His sisters laughed heartily, thinking him to be only in jest; but their amusement changed to wonder and admiration when, after running his fingers lightly over the keys, he began playing a soft and melodious prelude. It seemed that when a boy of fifteen, he had as a sort of amusement learned the rudiments of music, but he had not began with any settled purpose of making progress in the study, and had soon become tired of it. What then was their surprise to hear him sing with much taste and skill, to a beautiful accompaniment, a song he had learned in England.

He explained, that while in England, a class-mate of his, who was an excellent musician, had given him lessons; and that after a time he had become very fond of it, and had practised much during his leisure hours.

It was easy to see that Willie was almost idolized by all the family. During the evening Mrs. Leighton could scarcely take her eyes from the face of her son, and they all eagerly listened to his every word; and any one who saw the noble looking young man, could not wonder at their affection for him. When he rose from the piano, Birdie and Lewis begged for one more song, but Mrs. Leighton reminded them that it was late, and that their brother must be fatigued. And soon after prayers, the happy family separated for the night.

CHAPTER VI.

AN EVENING PARTY.

PREVIOUS to the return home of Laura and Willie, the Leighton's had seen but little company for a family of their wealth and social position; but now, instead of the heretofore quiet evenings, their superb parlors were thronged with acquaintances and friends, for both Willie and Laura had been favourites with both young and old.

Laura had intended giving a large party, but had deferred it till Willie should return home; and soon after his arrival the invitations were sent, and preparations were commenced for the contemplated party. I did not expect, neither did I wish, to be included among the guests. I had never attended a fashionable party in my life; and I thought, even were I favoured with an invitation, that I should feel strangely out of place amid so much display of wealth and fashion as I should be sure to meet with at a party given by one of the most wealthy and influential families in the city.

I was much surprised when I received from Laura

a very cordial invitation to attend her party. I at first declined the invitation, saying that I was unaccustomed to any thing of the kind, and that as most of the guests would be strangers to me, I should prefer not attending; but when Mr. and Mrs. Leighton expressed their wish that I should attend the party, I overcame my reluctance and consented.

The evening at length came, and although I anticipated but little pleasure from the party, I felt a degree of restlessness and expectation when the appointed evening arrived. My wardrobe was not furnished with any superfluities in the way of dress, and my command of money was not sufficient to allow of any extravagance in apparel. Laura kindly offered to present me with a beautiful silk dress for the occasion, but I delicately, though firmly, declined the gift, for I wished not to appear otherwise than in my true position. I therefore selected the most appropriate dress I possessed for the occasion, it was quite plain, though of rich material. The only ornament I wore was a pearl necklace, which had been a bridal gift to my mother.

Laura assisted me in making my toilette, and insisted that I should allow her to place a few natural flowers in my hair, and to please her I consented to wear them. Laura looked very lovely in the costly dress purchased for the occasion, she also wore a set of diamond ornaments, which her father had presented to her on her return from school.

As soon as we had finished our toilettes, we descended to the drawing room, where Mr. and Mrs. Leighton had already taken their places, as it was near the hour when they might expect their guests to begin to assemble.

I went down thus early to avoid the unpleasantness of entering the brilliantly lighted drawing-room after it should be filled with guests. I had requested of the Leightons that I might receive as few introductions as possible, under the circumstances. Truly it was a brilliant assembly which soon filled those spacious apartments. Among the guests who first arrived were a Mr. and Mrs. Lawton, with their daughter, to whom Laura gave me an introduction.

Their kind attentions and lively conversation soon dispelled the feeling of embarrassment with which I first found myself in the company of so many wealthy and distinguished people.

Dancing was soon introduced. Dancing was an accomplishment which I had never learned, as my mother disapproved of the amusement. Willie seemed disappointed when he invited me to become his partner for the quadrille then forming, and I replied that I did not dance. When he learned that I did not dance he introduced to me a young gentleman by the name of Shirley, who was seated near us, and who, for some reason or other, did not join the dancers. Mr. Shirley's conversational powers were extremely good, and we engaged in conversation for some time, in the course of which I enquired why he refrained from dancing? A shade of sadness passed over his countenance as he replied,—

"When a mere youth I was very fond of the amusement, and devoted much time to the practice of it. I believe it is the only thing which I ever knowingly did against the wishes of my parents; but my fondness for dancing amounted almost to a passion, and I often frequented the giddy ball-room when I knew that I was grieving my fond parents by so doing. My father and mother considered dancing a sinful amusement; but as my inclination to follow it was so strong, they finally forbore to admonish me further.

"When I was about twenty years of age my mother died. I was then residing at a distance from home. When mother's illness became alarming, I was summoned home. I was tenderly attached to my mother, and my grief was overwhelming when I saw that she must die. A short time before her death, she said to me one day, when we chanced to be left alone, 'My dear son, there is one subject upon which I wish to speak with you, 'ere I leave you for ever. You know I have ever considered dancing to be a sinful amusement. There may be no sin in the simple act of dancing, but it is an amusement which certainly has a tendency to evil. I know that you very much enjoy it, but you are now capable of serious reflection, and allow me to ask you if you feel in a suitable frame of mind for prayer and meditation when you retire to your room after having spent the evening in the frivolous amusement of dancing?' This was an argument which I could neither gainsay nor resist, and, coming as it did from the lips of my dying mother, I was much affected by it. Before leaving my mother's room I solemnly promised her that I would never again participate in the amusement of dancing, and that promise I have most sacredly kept. I now often wonder that I could ever have been so fond of an amusement which at the best affords so little real enjoyment to its votaries. I trust you will pardon the liberty which I have taken in talking so long of myself to you, an entire stranger; but when you enquired my reason for not joining in the dance, something in your countenance impelled me to be thus candid in my answer."

We remained for some time longer in conversation, and I really began to enjoy the party. There were several ladies and gentlemen seated near us, engaged also in conversation, and I could not avoid hearing much that passed among them. Presently I heard a lady enquire of a Mrs. Kingsley, a lady to whom I had been introduced in the early part of the evening,—

"Who is that young lady with whom Mr. Shirley has been so long conversing?"

"Oh!" she replied, "she is *only* the governess in Mrs. Leighton's family. A *person*, as I am informed, of good education, but very poor, and obliged to teach as a means of support for herself and mother, who is a widow."

Why should I have felt so indignant at those words, which, if maliciously intended, were certainly true? I suppose the attentions I was receiving at this my first party were causing me to forget my true position. The lady who had first spoken remarked further to Mrs. Kingsley,—

"Don't you think her very pretty—almost beautiful? I think I never before saw so intelligent a countenance."

Mrs. Kingsley replied,—

"I see nothing so very intelligent in her countenance, and if you consider her pretty, I must say that I am astonished at your taste; indeed I think her quite common-looking. I almost wonder that the Leightons should have made her a guest at a party with their friends; but then Miss Laura is kind-hearted, and I presume invited her out of pity —those *poor people* have so few pleasures."

The other lady replied,—

"Hush! She may hear you."

And they changed the subject. I had, however, heard quite enough to spoil my enjoyment for the rest of the evening. I was young and inexperienced then, and this was my first, though by no means my last, lesson in those distinctions which the world draws between the rich and the poor. Had I possessed a little more knowledge of the world I should better have understood the matter, knowing, as I did, that Mrs. Kingsley had an unmarried daughter present, of uncertain age, with a fair prospect of remaining for some time longer in her state of single blessedness. I forbear describing Miss Kingsley, and will only say that if Mrs. Kingsley thought me common-looking, I, on the contrary, thought her daughter, Miss Kinsgley, to be very uncommon-looking.

After the remarks to which I had been an unwilling listener, I derived very little pleasure from the party. I mentally said, if my poverty is to be made a subject of conversation in parties like this, I wish never to attend another; and I was heartily glad when the gay assembly departed, at two o'clock in the morning.

Thus ended my first party, which would have afforded me much enjoyment had I not chanced to hear those annoying remarks from Mrs. Kingsley.

The party given by the Leightons was soon succeeded by others among their numerous acquaintances. To several of those parties I was favored with invitations, which I invariably declined, for I had decided to attend no more fashionable parties. At length, when urged by the Leightons to give my reasons for steadily refusing all invitations, I informed them of the remarks I had overheard from Mrs. Kingsley on the night of Laura's party. Never shall I forget the look of scorn and contempt with which Willie Leighton listened as I related the circumstance; but he made no remark, as he knew Mrs. Kingsley to be one of his mother's most intimate friends. Mrs. Leighton remarked that Mrs. Kingsley possessed many good qualities, although she was sometimes inclined to make malicious remarks.

CHAPTER VII.

FAILING HEALTH OF CLARA'S MOTHER.

I SOON had a far more serious cause for disquiet than the remarks of Mrs. Kingsley or any one else could have occasioned. I had many times during the past year feared that my mother's health was failing. She looked thin and pale, and seemed to lack her usual activity in performing her household duties. I frequently enquired if she were ill, and she had ever replied that she was quite well; only it might be a little fatigued. But the truth could no longer be concealed. My mother was ill, and that seriously. She still attended to her daily occupations, but she was greatly changed; she seemed during the past few weeks to have grown thin almost to attenuation. She was very pale, except at times there was a feverish glow upon her cheeks. I was then too young to detect, as I should now do, the insidious approach of that foe to human life, consumption. Going one day to visit my mother, I was so struck by the change so visible in her countenance, I privately asked Aunt Patience if she did not feel alarmed for my mother? She burst into tears, and was for some time unable to reply. I had never before seen Aunt Patience so much affected. I begged of her to tell me if there was any real cause for alarm, for I had hoped she would be able to dispel all my fears in regard to my mother. Regaining her composure, she told me that consumption was hereditary in my mother's family. I had never before chanced to hear it mentioned, but Aunt Patience now informed me that several of the family had fallen victims to that disease, and that she feared it had already fastened upon my mother.

"I am glad," said she, "that you have spoken to me upon the subject. I have long wished to make known my feelings to you, but I shrank from giving you pain. I have been unable to persuade your mother to call a physician. She imagines herself better; but I can see but too plainly that such is not the case."

I forebore mentioning the subject to my mother at that time; indeed I could not have done so. I was now thoroughly alarmed—almost terrified, and it was with a heavy heart that I returned to the dwelling of Mrs. Leighton.

I had frequently spoken to Mrs. Leighton of my mother's failing health, and I now felt it my duty to resign my position as governess, for a time at least, and return to my mother, that she might be relieved from all care. When I returned to Mrs. Leighton's on the evening in question, I again spoke to her upon the subject, saying that I feared I should be obliged to resign my situation in her family, and return to my mother, who evidently needed my attention. Mrs. Leighton expressed much sympathy for me in my trouble, saying that I ought by all means to hasten to my mother; but added that she did not wish me to resign my position, as she was willing to wait for me for any length of time I might find it necessary to remain at home. She said, further, that Laura would be quite willing to give some attention to the children during my absence; and she tried to cheer me up, saying that she trusted my mother would soon be better. I too tried to be hopeful, but the impression that my mother was to die had taken deep hold of my mind.

I visited my mother the next evening, and, to avoid surprising her by suddenly returning home, I informed her that I intended spending a few weeks at home, as I needed rest from teaching, and that Laura would attend to the children during the time I should remain at home. My mother seemed so cheerful that evening that I began to hope that I might have been too much alarmed; but, when I had opportunity for speaking privately with Aunt Patience, her words confirmed my worst fears. She informed me that at her earnest solicitation my mother had that day summoned a physician; that he had prescribed some medicine, for her, and given her some advice in regard to diet, walking or riding in the open air, &c. She further informed me that she had herself spoken privately to the physician, requesting him to tell her candidly what he thought of my mother's case. He replied,—

"As you have asked me a plain question, I think it my duty to give you a candid answer. I know not," continued the physician, "how it might have been had I been called six months ago, but now I fear the case of Mrs. Roscom is beyond the reach of medicine. I will gladly do my utmost for her, but I fear that a few months, it may be a few weeks, will terminate her life."

This was *fearful* tidings to me, as I had strongly hoped that the opinion of the physician would have been more favorable. When I became outwardly composed, I rejoined my mother, in company with Aunt Patience. My mother was not aware that Aunt Patience had held any conversation with the physician regarding her illness. She seemed much pleased at the prospect of my return home. I informed her, before leaving, that she might expect my return in the course of two or three days.

She failed rapidly from this time; and, shortly

after I returned to my home, was obliged to give up all employment, however light. We often reminded her of the physician's wish, that she should walk in the open air; but it was seldom she felt equal to the task of walking even a short distance.

Mrs. Leighton and Laura often called, and brought many little delicacies to tempt the appetite of my invalid mother. Mrs. Leighton told my mother that she would be happy to send her carriage as often as she felt strong enough to ride out. My mother replied that in fine days she would gladly avail herself of her kind offer; and so, as long as my mother was able, the carriage was sent every fine day to give her the benefit of a short ride in the open air.

I presume that, on ordinary occasions, I should have felt some embarrassment in receiving a visit from Mrs. Leighton and Laura in my home, which appeared so humble, compared to their own elegant residence; but now it never cost me a thought, for, in the presence of a great sorrow, all trifling considerations vanish away.

It was in the month of May that I returned home, and by the last of June my mother was entirely confined to her room, and much of the time to her bed. She suffered much from nervous restlessness, and at times her cough was very distressing. She would allow no one, as yet, to sit with her during the night, but I gained her consent that I might sleep on a lounge which stood in her room.

There was no end to the kindness we received from the Leightons; no day passed without some one of the family calling to enquire for my mother.

Soon after this time my mother appeared much better. She was able to sit up more than formerly, and her cough was far less troublesome. I remember one day saying to Aunt Patience, when we chanced to be alone, that I began to think my mother would yet recover, she seemed so much better.

"My dear Clara," she replied, "I hope your mother may recover; but you must not build hopes which I fear will never be realized. This seeming change for the better is only one of those deceitful turns of her disease by which so many are deceived. I do not wish to alarm you needlessly, but I dare not cherish any hopes of her recovery."

The idea that my mother would die had been impressed upon my mind from the first; yet, when I observed her improved appearance, I thought that the physician, as well as ourselves, might have been deceived.

CHAPTER VIII.

A BRIGHT DREAM AND PEACEFUL END.

THE seeming favorable turn of my mother's disease proved, as Aunt Patience had feared, of but short duration. She was soon again almost entirely confined to her bed; except that, in the afternoons, for the sake of the change, she would recline for a short time upon the sofa in the parlor. But this was only for a few days, and then she was unable to leave her own apartment.

As I have said so little regarding my own feelings, in view of my mother's death, the reader may be led to think that I felt less keenly than I might have been supposed to do. If I have said little, it is for the reason that I have no words adequate to describe what my feelings were at the time. I felt stunned as by a heavy blow; and it seemed to me if my mother died I certainly could not live. I had yet to learn that grief does not kill—that is, not suddenly.

I have often since looked back to that time, and felt deeply humbled, while thinking how little I felt resigned to the will of heaven. I could not then, as

I have since done, recognize the hand of a kind and loving Father in the stroke. I could only feel that my mother was leaving me, and all was darkness beyond. I now scarcely ever left my mother's room, except when Aunt Patience would almost compel me, for a short time, to retire to my own apartment, that I might obtain a little rest. But the thought that soon I would have no mother was ever present to my mind, and I wished to remain with her as long as she might be spared to me.

About three weeks previous to my mother's death, Aunt Patience urgently requested me one afternoon to retire to my own room and seek some rest, saying I looked entirely worn out. After obtaining from her a promise that she would not allow me to sleep too long, I complied. My room seemed very cool and refreshing that sultry afternoon, and, lying down upon my bed, I soon sank into a profound slumber, which continued for three or four hours. Upon my going down stairs, I was surprised at the lateness of the hour, and enquired of Aunt Patience why she had not called me? She replied that as my mother had seemed quite comfortable, she thought it best to let me enjoy a sound sleep. I persuaded Aunt Patience to retire to rest soon after tea, as I intended watching that night by my mother. Thus far we had ourselves been able to attend to the wants of my mother, without assistance, as it pleased her better that either Aunt Patience or I should attend to her; but we had lately allowed a friend to sleep in the house, as we did not like to be left alone. That evening, after my mother had partaken of a little light refreshment, she seemed inclined to sleep. I took up a book and tried to become interested in its pages. As my mother now seemed to enjoy a peaceful slumber, I remember I thought her dreams must have been happy ones, for I often noticed a smile upon her countenance. I think she had slept nearly two hours, when she awoke, and requested me to give her a drink. I supported her upon my arm as I held to her lips a glass in which I had mixed some wine and water. Laying her gently back upon her pillows, I enquired if I could do anything further for her comfort? She replied that she felt quite comfortable; and, thinking that she might again fall asleep, I resumed my reading. After remaining quiet for some time she softly called my name. As I stepped hastily to her bed-side, she said,—

"Come and sit near me, Clara, I have something to say to you."

Obedient to her request, I drew my chair near to her bedside, and seated myself. She clasped my hand in both hers, as she said,—

"My dear Clara, I have long wished to ask you if you are aware that I must soon leave you?"

As she said these words the grief of my overburdened heart defied control, and, burying my face in her pillows, I sobbed convulsively. This sudden near approach to death sent an icy chill over my whole being.

"You must endeavor to compose yourself, my daughter," said my mother, "and listen to me."

I tried to restrain my tears as my mother continued.

"I have long wished to talk with you, but have deferred it from time to time, through fear of giving you pain; but I now feel it an imperative duty to converse with you upon the subject. Allow me to tell you a dream which visited me in the slumber from which I awoke a few minutes since. In my dream I seemed to be walking alone on a calm summer's evening, without any definite object in view. When I had walked for a considerable distance the scene suddenly changed, and I found myself walking by the banks of a placid river. Looking forward, I observed a person advancing to meet me, whom I at once knew to be your father. My joy was great at the prospect of meeting him; for, in my dream, I recollected that he had been long dead. I enquired of him how it happened that I met him there? He replied, 'I saw you coming when you were yet a long way off, and feared you might lose your way.' Turning back in the direction from whence he had come, he turned towards me, with a pleasant smile, and said, 'follow me.' As we walked onward, I observed that the river by which we walked seemed gradually to become more narrow the further we advanced. He continued to walk onward for some time, a little in advance of me, when suddenly stopping, he turned to me and said, 'My dear Alice, look across to the other side of the river, and behold the place which is now my home.' The breadth of the river had continued to lessen, till it was now only a narrow line of water which separated us from the opposite shore. I looked as he directed me, and, oh! Clara, I can find no words by which to describe to you what I saw. It so far surpassed anything pertaining to this world that I am unable to give you any description of it. I felt an intense desire to cross the narrow stream which separated me from that beautiful place. I enquired of your father if I could not with him cross the stream and enter those golden gates, which I could plainly see before me. He replied, 'No, my dear Alice, every one must cross this river *alone*. You must go back for a brief period, as you have yet a mission to perform before taking your final leave of earth. You must comfort the sorrowing heart of our child 'ere you leave her. Tell her of the home which I now inherit, where there is also a place prepared for you and for her, if you so live as to be found worthy to enter those gates which you see before you.' He then said, 'I must now leave you, and you must return to our Clara for a few brief days, when you will be summoned to rejoin me in yonder blissful abode.' I turned to make some further remark to him, but he had gone from my sight, and I awoke with my mind deeply impressed by my dream. But now," added my mother, to me, "the bitterness of death is already past. It is for you only that I grieve. I trust, however, that, instead of grieving immoderately for your mother, you will endeavor to discharge your duty in whatever position it may please God to place you, and so live that whenever you may be called from this world it may be to meet your mother in Heaven. Since my illness my mind has been much exercised regarding my own state as a sinner; for, be assured, Clara, that, in the near prospect of death, we find in ourselves much that is unworthy, which had before escaped our notice while in the enjoyment of health. But I am now happy while I tell you that all is peace with me. I now feel willing to depart whenever it is the will of my Heavenly Father to call me hence, and I feel confident that in a very few days I shall be summoned from earth. I am sorry to see you grieve," said my mother, for I was weeping bitterly; "endeavor to derive consolation from what I have said, and be thankful that when I leave you it will be to rejoin your dear father where there is neither sorrow nor sighing."

Seeing that my tears agitated my mother, I succeeded in checking them, and assumed an air of composure, which I was far from feeling. After the above conversation with me, my mother enjoyed a night of tranquil repose. I now felt the certainty of her death, and prayed for strength to meet the sorrow which that event would bring to me.

So calm and peaceful were the last days of my mother's life that we could hardly recognize the presence of the King of Terrors, till the damps of death were gathering upon her brow. She died at sunset on a mild evening in September. She had passed the day almost entirely free from pain. Toward evening she slept for an hour; on waking, she said to me,—

"My dear child, I think the hour of my departure has arrived. I feel that I am dying."

I now observed that look upon the countenance of my mother which tells us that a loved friend is no longer ours. She requested me to call Aunt Patience, which I instantly did. I also sent a hasty summons to her physician, although it was needless, for she was even then entering the dark valley. The physician soon arrived, and, after one look at my mother, said to me, in a low voice,—

"My dear Miss Roscom, as a physician, I can be of no further use, but, as a friend, I will remain with you."

The physician was an old and valued friend, being the same who had stood by the death-bed of my father, and he deeply sympathized with me in this, my second bereavement.

As I stood by my mother, my grief was not noisy; it was far too deep and powerful for that. Outwardly, I was quite calm. My mother had endeavoured to prepare my mind for this hour. I had also prayed for strength to meet it with fortitude and resignation; but those who have stood by the dying bed of a fond mother may understand my sorrow. My mother was spared much of the suffering which attends the last moments of many. She seemed to be softly breathing her life away. After laying for some time tranquil and quiet, she suddenly opened her eyes and looked from one to the other of us. As they rested upon me, she made a sign that I should go nearer to her.

"Weep not, my dear child," said she, in a whisper; "be faithful, and you will yet meet me in heaven."

She also addressed a few words of like import to Aunt Patience. Suddenly, she raised her hands, and, as she looked upward, with a smile upon her countenance, we heard a sigh—and her spirit had returned unto God who gave it.

I was borne from the apartment in a state of insensibility, and, when I awoke to consciousness, the doctor and Aunt Patience were standing at my bedside. After administering a quieting draught, the physician left us, saying to Aunt Patience that she must try and induce me to sleep, as that would help to restore my shattered nerves. Aunt Patience sat by me during the long hours of that night, but it was not until the day began to dawn that I sank into a heavy slumber, from which I did not awake until a late hour in the morning. On first awaking, it seemed to me that I had had a frightful dream; but, as my mind became more clear, I realized the sad truth that my mother was no more. I heard a footstep enter my room, and soon a familiar voice addressed me, saying,—

"My dear Clara, I have come to see if I can be of any assistance to you in your sorrow."

It was Mrs. Leighton who had thus entered my room, she having hastened to our dwelling as soon as she learned of my mother's death. I could not at first reply to her kind words; I could only weep.

She did not force me to talk, but, gently, as a mother could have done, did she bathe my fevered brow and throbbing temples. Telling me to remain quiet for a few moments, she left the room, and soon returned, bearing a cup of tea, which she insisted upon my drinking. She assisted me to dress, and opened a window to admit the cool morning air. I tearfully thanked her for those kind attentions. She insisted that I should lean upon her for support, as we descended the stairs, and indeed I felt scarcely able to walk without assistance.

On going below, I found several kind friends, who had remained with Aunt Patience to render their assistance in any office of friendship we might require. Mrs. Leighton accompanied me to the room where lay the lifeless remains of my mother. I folded back the snowy napkin which covered her face, and gazed long upon those dear features, now stamped with the seal of death. As I gazed upon her now peaceful countenance, I felt that to wish her back again would be almost a sin. I also derived much comfort from the consoling words of Mrs. Leighton. I cannot dwell longer upon these sorrows. When I stood at my mother's grave, and looked down upon her coffin, after it had been lowered into the earth, I almost wished that I too were resting by her side. Since that period I have experienced other sorrows; but the sharpest pang I have ever felt, was when I turned away from the graves where rested the remains of both father and mother.

As I have before mentioned, Aunt Patience had, in the course of her life, passed through many trying vicissitudes; and, previous to her death, my mother had considered that we could make no better return for the debt of gratitude we owed her than by making provision for her old age. I say, with good reason, that we owed her a debt of gratitude, for, during her residence with us, she had shown the utmost kindness to both my mother and myself. And when my mother's health failed her, the care and attentions of Aunt Patience were unceasing. With a view of making provision for Aunt Patience, my mother had made arrangements that our house should be sold, and the money deposited for her future benefit. In making this arrangement, my mother wished me to accept of a portion of the money which the sale of the house would bring; but I declined, saying that, as she had given me a good education, I was amply able to support myself, so long as I was blessed with health. My mother assented to the arrangement, saying that I could draw money from the deposit should I ever have occasion so to do.

We remained for two months in our lonely home, after the death of my mother; at the end of which time the new owner took possession of the dwelling. Aunt Patience had decided upon going to reside with a relative who lived in Massachusetts, and the interest of the money, deposited for her use, was to be regularly remitted to her. We disposed of the furniture, with the exception of a few cherished articles, which I reserved for myself; these the purchaser kindly allowed me to leave in one of the upper rooms till I might wish to remove them. The same day that Aunt Patience set out on her journey to Massachusetts, I returned to Mrs. Leighton.

CHAPTER IX.

FRIENDLY ATTENTIONS.

IT was well for me that my mind was actively employed; had it been otherwise I should have continually brooded over my sorrows. As it was, when engaged with my duties in the school-room, my thoughts would wander to those two graves in the church-yard, and my tears would fall upon the book from which I was listening to a recitation from my pupils. Georgania having left home, I had only Birdie and Lewis as pupils. Much pity did those affectionate children evince for me when they could not but observe my grief. Birdie would often say,—

"Please, Miss Roscom, do not grieve so much; we all love you dearly, and will be very kind to you."

And Lewis, who could never bear to see my tears, would say,—

"I will be a little brother to you, Miss Roscom, so please don't cry any more."

To please my pupils, I endeavored to appear cheerful; but truly the heart knoweth its own bitterness. One thought, however, afforded me some consolation, and that was, that I was obeying my mother's dying injunction, by striving to do my duty in the position in which I was placed. As days and months passed away, I, in some measure, regained my usual cheerfulness, although I was nowise inclined to forget my mother.

A year had now passed since I saw her laid in the grave. I often visited her resting-place, and there renewed my resolve to follow her precepts; and many a time, kneeling by her grave, did I implore wisdom from on high to enable me to follow the counsels I had so often received from those lips, now sealed in silence. It seemed to me, at such times, that I almost held communion with the spirit of my mother.

I experienced much kindness from every member of Mr. Leighton's family I spent my leisure time mostly in my room. They did not, of course, invite me to join parties, but they would often urge me to join a few friends in their own parlor; but I always replied that my deep mourning must be my excuse. I had no taste for company or mirth.

One afternoon the Leightons had gone to join a pic-nic party some two miles from the city. They had invited me to accompany them, but, as usual, I declined. I felt sad and lonely that long afternoon, and, being left entirely alone, I could not prevent my thoughts from recurring to the past. I thought of all the happy, careless days of my childhood; then my memory ran back to the night when, at ten years of age, I stood by the death-bed of my father. With the eye of memory, I again saw my mother, as she stood bowed with grief at the grave of my father; and now I was left alone to mourn for both father and mother. Memory also fondly turned to Miss Edmonds, my first teacher. I felt that to see her again would indeed be happiness; but I knew not where Miss Edmonds then resided. The last time I had heard from her she contemplated going South, as governess in a gentleman's family. Then came the memory of the happy years I passed in Mrs. Wentworth's school. Where now were the many friends I had then known and loved? As these thoughts passed in quick succession through my mind, I could not refrain from weeping; and, as I was under no restraint from the presence of others, my tears seemed almost a luxury. I know not how long my fit of weeping might have continued had not one of the domestics entered the room, and informed me that a poor woman was in the kitchen seeking charity.

"I thought," said the girl, "as the other ladies

are all away, you might give her a trifle, for she seems very needy."

Hastily drying my tears, I went down to the kitchen, where I found a young woman, who would have been very pretty but for the look of want and suffering depicted upon her countenance. It was evident, from her appearance, that she was not an habitual beggar. As I approached her, she seemed much embarrassed, as she said,—

"Sure an' its mesilf that never expected to come to this at all, at all."

"My poor woman," said I, "you appear to have been unfortunate."

"An' its mesilf that has been misfortunate," she replied, as the tears gathered in her fine, dark eyes. She continued,—

"There was never a happier couple than Dinnis O'Flaherty an' I the day the praste made us one. But, after a while, the wages got low, and the times were hard wid us. 'Polly,' says Dinnis to me one day, 'will you be afther goin' to Ameriky wid me?' 'Dinnis,' says I, 'wherever it plases you to go its I, Polly McBrine, that's ready and willin' to follow.' We sailed in the *St. Pathrick*, and tin days afther I saw my darlin' Dinnis buried in the salt say. He fell sick wid a faver, and all me prayers for his life could not save him; an' here I am, a lone widdy, in a shtrange land, without a penny in me pocket, nor a place to lay me head."

Here the poor woman's grief choked her utterance, and, covering her face with her hands, she wept aloud. I requested the domestic to bring her some food, which she ate like one famishing. I placed in her hand money sufficient to secure her from want for two or three days at least. I did not in the least doubt her story, for her countenance bore the impress of sincerity. When she left, I requested her to call again in two or three days, as I felt certain that Mrs. Leighton would assist her in obtaining some employment. She left me with many thanks, and blessing me after the manner of her country.

CHAPTER X.

A SURPRISE.

AFTER tea I felt that I must walk out in the air, as I was suffering from a severe headache. I made my way to the church-yard, and sought the graves of my parents; and, seating myself at the headstone of my mother's grave, I remained for a long time wrapped in profound meditation.

I know not how long I remained thus, for I took no note of time; but when I raised my head at the sound of approaching footsteps, the shades of evening were gathering around me. It was Willie Leighton whose footsteps had aroused me from my reverie.

"My dear Clara," he began.

But when I looked up with a little surprise at his familiar use of my christian name, it being the first time he had thus addressed me, he colored slightly, and said,—

"I beg pardon, Miss Roscom, for thus intruding upon your solitude, but, finding you absent on our return, I came to seek you and, with your permission, to escort you home. I think you do wrong to come to this lonely place to cherish a sorrow which seems to me to be almost unreasonable. I would not have you forget your parents; but, surely, if they are permitted to look down upon you from their home in heaven, they would not wish to see you thus debar yourself from society and all the innocent pleasures of youth. The dews of evening," said he, "are beginning to fall, and I must insist upon your return home."

On our way home I could not help a feeling of uneasiness lest Willie's attentions to me should displease the family. I had allowed him to accompany me home, as I could not have done otherwise, without absolute rudeness; yet I feared that, in so doing, I should displease his friends. My uneasiness increased as, upon entering the house, I thought I detected a shade of displeasure in the manner of Mrs. Leighton toward me. If Willie noticed anything of the kind, he *seemed* unconscious of it, for he made several efforts to engage us in conversation; but, for some reason or other, no one, except himself, seemed inclined to be social that evening. I felt very much depressed in spirits, for I attributed their silence to displeasure because Willie had accompanied me home, and, at an early hour, I bade them good night, and retired to my own apartment. After reading, as was my custom, a chapter in my bible, and commending myself to the care of Heaven, I sought my pillow; but hour after hour passed away and sleep refused to visit my eyes. Again and again I mentally asked myself what had I done to merit the coldness which Mrs. Leighton had shown in her manner to me? It was not my fault that Willie had sought me, and in a kind and gentlemanly manner escorted me home; and I only attributed his attention to that respect which the *real* gentleman ever accords to a lady, be she rich or poor. I, however, decided that in future I should receive no attentions from Willie. The Leightons were kind, but extremely proud, and I feared that the pleasure Willie had lately evinced in my society had displeased them, although his attentions had been nothing more than a person socially inclined might be expected to show to one dwelling beneath the same roof. Again did the remark made by Mrs. Kingsley occur to my mind, and I firmly decided that, if Mrs. Leighton was displeased, she should have no further cause for displeasure, for I too was possessed of a proud spirit. The dawn of the new day glimmered in the east 'ere sleep closed my eyes, and then my slumbers were disturbed by unpleasant dreams. One dream, in particular, I still remember. I seemed, in my dream, to be a homeless wanderer I know not whither. I had left the limits of the city and was walking in the open country, on a road that seemed strange and unfamiliar to me. At length such a feeling of loneliness and misery overpowered me that I felt unable to proceed further. Seating myself by the roadside, I burst into tears. Raising my eyes, I observed a female figure approaching me, which I soon recognized as my mother. She drew near, and, laying her hands upon my head, as if in blessing, said,—

"Fear not, my beloved daughter, only continue in the path of duty and all will yet be well."

With a cry of joy, I sprang forward to embrace her, and awoke to find the sun shining dimly through the partially closed blinds of my window. I felt fatigued and nervous, after passing such a restless night. I was startled by the pale and haggard countenance which my mirror reflected that morning. I had scarcely finished my toilet when the breakfast bell rung, and I hastened down stairs, where the family were already assembled around the breakfast table.

Whatever of displeasure Mrs. Leighton might have felt the previous evening seemed to have vanished with the light of morning. Perhaps, thought I, her displeasure existed only in my own imagination, after all. Noticing my pale countenance, she enquired if I was ill? I replied that I had a slight headache, owing to my not having slept well. She kindly offered to excuse me from attending to my pupils that morning, but I told her that I felt quite able to attend to my usual duties. In the course of the day I mentioned to her the case of the poor woman who had called the day previous. She replied that, after seeing her and making some enquiries regarding her capability, she would speak to a friend of hers, who was in want of a servant, and she had no doubt she could influence her friend to engage her, should she consider her a suitable person. Accordingly, when Mrs. O'Flaherty called, two or three days after, Mrs. Leighton questioned her in regard to her capability as a servant. She replied that she had had considerable experience as a servant in genteel families, previous to her marriage in the old country. Mrs. Leighton requested her to call again shortly, saying that she hoped to be able to find her a situation. Mrs. Leighton further informed her that, if the lady engaged her, it must be entirely on her own recommendation; and that she hoped she would prove herself faithful and trustworthy. She replied,—

"An' its mesilf that'll be afther doin' me best to plaze the leddy, mem."

And, with many thanks, she left the house. Mrs. Leighton was much interested by the intelligent countenance and honest, truthful manner of the woman, and she accordingly so strongly enlisted the sympathies of her friend, Mrs. Wallingford, that she agreed to give her a trial. Mrs. O'Flaherty seemed very thankful when she called, soon after, and Mrs. Leighton informed her that she had obtained a situation for her. Mrs. Leighton also furnished her with money sufficient to purchase some plain, but decent clothing, and a few days after she entered upon her duties in the dwelling of Mrs. Wallingford, who afterwards frequently remarked to Mrs. Leighton that she had much reason to thank her for providing her with the best servant she had ever engaged.

CHAPTER XI.

EMBARRASSING INTERVIEWS.

MY time passed in the usual daily routine of duties. About this time Georgania returned to spend a few weeks at home. Though much improved in personal appearance, she was far from being a pleasant companion. Her manner, to me, was exceedingly haughty, almost contemptuous. She seemed to have entirely forgotten my unwearied pains in laying the foundation of her education. I could never understand the reason of her dislike to me. The feeling must always have existed, though kept in check during the time she had been my pupil. I think the rest of the family must have noticed her unpleasant manner to me; and, I have no doubt, remonstrated with her upon the subject. I was of a proud, sensitive nature, and the many slights, in an indirect way, which I suffered from her roused my indignation, and I was revolving the idea in my mind of seeking another home, when an event occurred which caused my departure from the home of the Leightons sooner than I anticipated. On the morning of the day of which I speak, Laura was unable to go out, as she was suffering from a cold. She was very anxious to execute some shopping that morning, and asked me if I would undertake to make her purchases, as I knew exactly what she wanted. I gladly assented, and, as I passed the sitting-room, on my way up stairs, I heard Willie say,—

"I too have business up town, and I will drive Miss Roscom to the store where she is to make her purchases, and call for her on my return."

Mrs. Leighton replied in a low, but changed voice,—

"Why not send James, the coachman; it is more proper."

I did not wait to hear Willie's reply, but, when I came down, prepared for going out, the coachman was in waiting with the carriage. I was glad that Willie was not to accompany me, for, since the evening he had escorted me home, I had carefully avoided his society.

I was sitting that evening in the garden, in a kind of arbor, covered with creeping vines. I was deeply interested in the volume I held in my hand, and was much surprised when Willie suddenly entered the arbor, and took a seat by my side. I made a hasty movement to rise and leave the arbor, when he addressed me, saying,—

"Why is it, Miss Roscom, that you constantly avoid me, and treat me with such marked coolness? I am sure I have not merited such treatment. I have long sought an opportunity to speak with you alone, and now you must hear me. Allow me to tell you that I have long loved you, with a deep and true affection. Will you not become my wife, and thereby render me the happiest of mortals?"

I was so much surprised by this unexpected declaration that it was some moments before I could collect my thoughts sufficiently to reply. I at length said,—

"Although deeply sensible of the honor you have done me, I must say, in reply, that I can never become your wife."

He regarded me with unfeigned surprise as he said,—

"Then you do not love me, Clara. I had hoped that I was not wholly indifferent to you."

I replied,—

"As I believe you have addressed me with candour, I will answer you in the same manner. I do love you; and, were I guided by my own heart in the matter, my reply to your honorable proposal would have been different. But there are insurmountable barriers to our union."

"Name them," was his reply.

"Mr. Leighton," I answered. "Whether or not

you are aware of the fact I am unable to say; but *I know* that your family would never consent to your marriage with their governess. They may respect and treat me kindly in my present position, but would never be willing to receive me as a daughter. It will, therefore, be wiser for you to place your affections upon some one in your own position in life."

"Am I not," replied Willie, "free to follow my own wishes in the matter? What care I for those butterflies of fashion, whose highest enjoyment is to shine in the gay assembly or crowded ball-room. My heart's devotion must be given to one who possesses true nobility of mind. Should my parents refuse their consent to our marriage, then shall I feel justified in following the dictates of my own heart. I have never disobeyed my parents, and have endeavored to be guided by their counsels, but in this matter I must act in accordance with my own affection and judgment. In everything except wealth you are my equal, and I have enough for us both. Allow me to tell my parents that my happiness rests upon their consent to our marriage; and, should they withhold their consent, I will marry you and abide the consequences, for I am certain they will soon be sensible of their error." Being anxious to terminate the interview, I replied,—

"I must answer you, Mr. Leighton, in the manner which I consider will be best for us both. Never will I consent to become the wife of any man, and, by so doing, alienate him from his parents. I have experienced nothing but kindness from all your family, and I cannot take a step which will bring sorrow and disquiet into your heretofore happy home. Be advised by me and never allude to this subject again. I can be your friend, but not your wife. I intend, as soon as circumstances permit, to seek another home. Remember me as a friend only, and whatever my own feelings may be, I shall at least have the satisfaction of knowing that I have acted wisely and for the best."

His countenance expressed extreme agitation, as, rising, he said,—

"You have made me very unhappy, Miss Roscom. I will remain silent for the present; but go not away from here, as that would destroy my only hope."

When I entered the house, I heard the excited voices of Mrs. Leighton, Laura, and Georgania in the parlor. I heard Mrs. Leighton say, as I passed the door of the parlor,—

"Are you sure, Georgania, that you understood aright?"

"Quite sure, mamma," she replied; I plainly heard Willie ask her to become his wife; how I *hate* her; and the thought of Willie's loving her almost causes me to hate him."

"Hush!" exclaimed Mrs. Leighton; "I will investigate this matter myself."

I hurried up to my room. I knew there was trouble in store for me, and I felt strong to meet it; for my own conscience acquitted me of any wrong-doing. After some little time had passed, I heard the footsteps of Mrs. Leighton ascending the stairs; and a moment after she rapped at my door. I opened the door and invited her to enter, and be seated. She then seated herself, and sat for some moments in silence. Her countenance expressed both sorrow and anger, for, up to this time, I believed that Mrs. Leighton had loved me. I waited for Mrs. Leighton to open the subject, for I well knew what had brought her to my room, and I cared not how soon she made known the object of her visit. At length she said,—

"It seems to me, Miss Roscom, that you have rendered a very base return for my kindness."

As she seemed waiting my reply, I said,—

"Will you have the goodness, Mrs. Leighton, to explain your words, for I am unable to comprehend their meaning?"

Her voice expressed much displeasure as she answered:

"I was not aware that my words required any explanation; but, if they do, it shall be given in few words. How dare you so far forget your own position, and ours, as to entice my son into making a proposal of marriage to one so much his inferior as you must know yourself to be?"

Should I live a hundred years I can never forget the shock her words gave me. I fairly trembled with anger. Rising to my feet, I looked her steadily in the face, as I said,—

"That your words are false, as well as heartless, I need not tell you, as you are already aware of the fact. I appeal to you if I have ever in any way courted the society of Willie. If he has asked me to become his wife, is it through any fault of mine? But you need give yourself no uneasiness upon the subject, for I have already told Willie that I will never become the wife of any man whose friends would look upon me as their inferior. For, though poor, and obliged to labor for my bread, I possess a spirit equally proud with your own, and that spirit your insulting words have roused. When you accuse me of enticing Willie into making a proposal of marriage, you well know that your accusation is false and without foundation."

"I suppose," said Mrs. Leighton, after a short

silence, "that you will see the propriety of seeking another home."

"You might," I replied, "have spared yourself the trouble of reminding me of this, as I intend, this night, to leave your house. I intend to show you that I shall prove no hindrance to your son's marrying in accordance with your wishes. Allow me to express my heart-felt thanks for your past kindness to me; but we must now part."

Mrs. Leighton's anger, by this time, was beginning to cool.

"I am perfectly willing," said she, "that you should remain here till you can obtain another situation. When I spoke of your seeking another home, I wished not that you should understand that I wished you to leave immediately."

I thanked her, but said "I preferred going at once."

She enquired whither I intended going? I replied that there were several families residing in the city who had known and loved my mother, who would gladly shelter her orphan daughter.

Mrs. Leighton owed me, at the time, one hundred dollars of my salary; as I had not required the money, I had left it in her hands. Leaving the room, she soon returned with the money in her hand, and pressed me to accept of fifty dollars over and above what was owing me. I thanked her, but said I wished to accept only of what was my just due. As she refused to receive back the money, I laid it upon the table, and began making my preparations for leaving her house. In less than an hour my trunks were packed, and I was ready to go. Laura and Georgania, I think purposely, avoided me, for I did not see them before leaving. I felt grieved when I parted with Birdie and Lewis, for I had become strongly attached to them. Lewis used often to say that boys never ought to cry; crying, he said, was only for girls and babies; but he must have forgotten himself on this occasion, for he cried bitterly when I bade him good-bye. As I turned from my pupils, Mrs. Leighton came forward and extended her hand to me. I could not refuse the hand that had so often administered to the wants of my dying mother. Neither of us uttered a word. We shook hands in silence, and I passed from the house, and entered the carriage which was in waiting for me. There was a family by the name of Burnside, with whom I had been intimate from childhood; to them I intended going, and in a few minutes I was set down at their door.

It chanced to be Mrs. Burnside herself who answered my ring at the door. In a few brief words I informed her of the circumstances which had caused me to leave Mrs. Leighton so suddenly; at the same time, asking her if she was willing to afford me a home for a short time, till I could obtain another situation?

"My dear Clara," she replied, "to my home you are freely welcome for any length of time you may wish to remain. To-morrow we will talk further of the matter, but not another word to-night, for you look very much fatigued."

The family consisted of Mr. and Mrs. Burnside, and an aunt of Mrs. Burnside's, who resided with them. They had two daughters, but they had both married and removed a long distance from their early home. Mrs. Burnside offered to conduct me to my room, which offer I gladly accepted, for I wished to be alone. The excitement which had sustained me through the events of the past few hours had now subsided; and, when left alone in my room, I sat down to reflect calmly upon my situation. I could not but feel justified in the step I had taken; but I could not avoid a feeling of uneasiness when I reflected that I was now homeless. I did not wish to remain long with Mrs. Burnside, as I well knew they would accept of no compensation from me; and, for that reason, I felt the necessity of obtaining another situation as soon as possible; but I could come to no decision till after conversing with

Mrs. Burnside upon the subject. After kneeling and imploring the protection and guidance of my Heavenly Father, I retired to rest, and, as I was worn out by the exciting events of the evening, sleep soon furnished a welcome relief from all anxious thoughts.

I was greeted kindly by Mr. and Mrs. Burnside the next morning, when we met at the breakfast table. The aunt, being somewhat of an invalid, did not usually take her morning meal with the family. The only allusion to my circumstances was made by Mr. Burnside, who said I had better defer any conversation upon the subject for the present, and that, in the meantime, he wished me to consider his house as my home.

About eleven o'clock that morning, as I was sitting in the room with Mrs. Russell, Mrs. Burnside's aunt, the servant came up to inform me that a young gentleman was in the parlor, who wished to see me. Looking at the card which the girl handed me, I read the name of Willie Leighton. I was sorry to wound his feelings; but, when I left their dwelling, I firmly resolved that I would never intentionally meet with Willie again. I therefore requested the servant to inform Mr. Leighton that I was engaged. It was no easy matter for me to send this message to *him*; but my pride sustained me.

Two or three weeks passed quietly away. During this time, Birdie and Lewis twice came to see me, but whether by permission or by stealth I could not determine, and I would not enquire. Willie called repeatedly, but I never granted him an interview, as I deemed it best for both that we should not meet.

I shall never cease to remember with gratitude the kindness I received from Mr. and Mrs. Burnside, and, as I wished not to abuse their hospitality, I thought it advisable, when some two months had passed away, to devise some means of earning my own support. They would have assisted me in obtaining a situation in Philadelphia; but I wished to leave my native city, and see if new scenes and new friends would not have a beneficial effect upon my mind. I had now no remaining tie to bind me to Philadelphia. I grieved, it is true, at the thought of leaving the place which contained the graves of my parents. Nevertheless, I felt myself to be in the path of duty, while preparing to leave my native city.

CHAPTER XII.

A NEW ENGLAND HOME.

I KNEW I had an uncle living in the State of New Hampshire, whom I had not seen since I was twelve years of age—he having visited us at that time. He was my mother's only brother, and to him I decided to go. I once thought of going to Aunt Patience, but finally gave up the idea. I retained a very distinct recollection of my uncle. I remembered that he and my mother had strongly resembled each other, although he was ten years her senior. When quite young he had married a very worthy woman, and their union was blessed by two children, a son and daughter; but they had laid them both in the grave at an early age; therefore they were now childless. I had never seen my aunt, but my heart turned toward them, and my resolution was soon taken to visit them. They resided about three miles from the village of Littleton, in New Hampshire.

The only obstacle in the way of my wishes was the long journey from Philadelphia to New Hampshire. I felt reluctant to undertake so long a journey alone. This obstacle was unexpectedly removed by the arrival of a Mr. and Mrs. Egmont, from the State of Ohio; they were relatives of Mrs. Burnside, and were journeying to the Eastern States, to visit some friends who resided there. Mr. Burnside mentioned to them my desire to visit my uncle in New Hampshire, and they gladly consented that I should accompany them on their journey. As they intended remaining but a few days in Philadelphia, I was obliged to hasten the preparations for my departure.

I could not but observe the hand of a kind Providence in directing Mr. and Mrs. Egmont to visit Philadelphia at this particular time.

On the evening preceding my departure I paid a farewell visit to the graves of my parents, and I shed some very bitter tears when I reflected that I might never again stand by this loved spot. I exacted a promise from Mrs. Burnside that, should any of the Leightons make enquiries concerning me, she would not inform them of my destination.

We left Philadelphia at a very early hour the next morning, and, after a very long and somewhat tedious journey, arrived in safety at the busy village of Littleton. Mr. Egmont conducted me to an hotel till he could make the necessary enquiries for finding my uncle. I knew he resided about three miles from the village, but was unable to say in what direction. Mrs. Egmont invited me to accompany them to their friends, who lived in the village, and rest before seeking my uncle; but, as I had arrived so near the termination of my journey, I wished to reach the home of my uncle without further delay. After accompanying Mrs. Egmont to their friends, Mr. Egmont returned to the hotel, where I awaited him. I was seated near a window, in the sitting-room, and heard him making enquiries of one and another for Mr. Wayland, my uncle. No one seemed to know anything of the person he sought. As the landlord passed that way, he turned to him and enquired if he knew a farmer in that vicinity by the name of Wayland? He replied that, having resided only for a short time in Littleton, his acquaintance did not, as yet, extend beyond the limits of the village, and that he knew of no such person. I was beginning to fear that my uncle had removed to some other place, as I had not heard anything from him for a considerable time, when a ragged-looking boy, apparently about twelve years of age, made his way up to Mr. Egmont, and said,—

"I can tell you where Mr. Wayland lives. He lives about three miles from here, on the Waterford Road. I knows you see, for I worked for him this fall, pickin' pertaters."

Giving the boy a piece of silver as he thanked him for his information, Mr. Egmont came to inform me that, when I had partaken of the dinner he had ordered for me, he would accompany me to the home of my uncle.

The lad before mentioned had given Mr. Egmont so accurate a description of my uncle's residence that, when we came in view of the square, old-fashioned farm-house described by the boy, we at once knew it to be my uncle's home. As we came in sight of the house, the question—how will they receive me?—arose in my mind; but the recollection which I retained of my uncle was of so pleasing a character that I had little doubt of meeting with a cordial welcome. As we drew near, I observed an elderly-looking man in the yard, engaged in mending some farming implement. From the appearance of the place, it seemed that the front entrance was but little used, the front door and blinds being closely shut. I was at that time wholly unacquainted with the habits and customs of country people. As we drove up to the gate, the man I had before observed paused in his employment, and regarded us, as I thought, with no little surprise. Surely, thought I, this man cannot be my Uncle Wayland. At the time of his visit to my mother he was a young and fine-looking man; but the man I now beheld was bowed as it were by age, and his hair was nearly white. I should have remembered that since I had seen him he had laid both of his loved children in the grave. True it is that sorrow causes premature old age; but, upon a second look at his countenance, I could clearly trace his resemblance to my mother. His eyes, when he raised them to look at us, so strongly resembled hers that my own filled with tears, which I hastily wiped away.

Alighting from the carriage, Mr. Egmont addressed my uncle, saying,—

"Have I the pleasure of speaking to Mr. Wayland?"

He replied in the affirmative, and added,—

"I know not whether or not I am addressing an old acquaintance; but your countenance is not familiar to me."

Mr. Egmont replied,—

"I am not aware that we have ever met before; but this young lady, who is your niece, Miss Roscom, has travelled in company with myself and wife, and I wished to leave her in your home before resigning my care of her."

My uncle seemed overjoyed at seeing me. He assisted me to alight, and embraced me with true affection. He immediately conducted me into the house, and introduced me to my aunt. She was a middle-aged, kindly-looking woman; and I also received from her a very cordial welcome to their home. They invited Mr. Egmont to remain till after tea, but he declined, saying that he had promised to return to their friends as soon as possible. After some conversation with my uncle and aunt, they advised me to retire to my room and seek rest, after the fatigues of my long journey; and I gladly followed my aunt up the stairs, to a neat bedroom, tastefully furnished. I was weary both in body and mind, and, lying down upon my bed, I soon sunk into a sound sleep. When I awoke, daylight was rapidly fading before the shadows of evening. I hastened down stairs, fearful that I had kept my uncle and aunt waiting for their tea. I enquired of my aunt if such were the case? She replied, saying,—

"I gave the hired men their suppers at the usual hour, but your uncle and I have waited to take our tea with you."

Can it be possible, thought I, that they take their meals with their hired servants? I had yet to learn the different usages of life in the city of Philadelphia and in a farm-house in the New England States. I wisely said nothing to my aunt of what was passing in my mind. Tea being over, we passed the remainder of the evening in social conversation. We had much to say, mutually, of family matters. I told them many particulars connected with the death of my mother, of which I had never informed them by letter. They also told me much concerning their deceased children. Their son had died at the age of fifteen. As he had a decided taste for books, my uncle intended giving him an education, instead of training him to the life of a farmer. For a year previous to his death he attended school in Massachusetts. Returning home to spend his vacation, his parents thought his health was impaired, but attributed it to hard study, for he was naturally studious. They were hopeful that relaxation from study, with exercise in the open air, would soon restore him to his usual health. But their hopes were not to be realized; even then had death marked him for his prey; and consumption, which was hereditary in his father's family, soon laid him in the grave. Three months after the grave had closed over their beloved son, Walter, their daughter, Caroline, fell a victim to a malignant fever, which at that time prevailed in the neighbourhood, and they saw her too laid in the grave, at the early age of twelve years—thus leaving them childless and sorrowing. We shed many tears while conversing of our mutual sorrows; and it was quite a late hour for the simple habits of their household when we separated for the night.

CHAPTER XIII.

NEW OCCUPATIONS.

WHEN going down stairs the next morning, I was surprised, the hour was so early, at finding my uncle and aunt, with their two farm servants, already seated at the breakfast table. I must confess that these two farm servants seemed to me strangely out of place, sitting thus familiarly at the same table with their master and mistress. My uncle introduced them to me, by the names of Mr. Barnes and Mr. Hawkins, their Christian names being Solomon and Obadiah, and by those names they were mostly called in my uncle's family. Solomon was a good humored looking man of some thirty years of age; he had, I afterwards learned, been for some years in my uncle's employ. Obadiah was a youth of about seventeen years of age. His extreme bashfulness in the presence of strangers in general, and of ladies in particular, caused him to appear very awkward. Added to this, he was, to use a common term, very homely in his personal appearance. His hair was very light, almost white; his eyes too were of a very light color, and uncommonly large and prominent. He was also freckled, and very much sun-burned. He seemed very much overgrown, and his general appearance suggested the idea that he must be in his own way—a position of which he seemed painfully conscious. He had a most unpleasant habit of keeping his eyes constantly in motion. As I was seated directly opposite to him at the breakfast table, I found it very difficult to restrain my inclination to laughter, for I could not raise my eyes without encountering one of those furtive glances. The idea occurred to me that he was meditating on some means of escape from the table, and it was with much difficulty that I maintained a becoming gravity. I was very glad, however, when my uncle made some remark which provoked a general laugh; but I am ashamed to acknowledge that I looked to see what effect a smile would have upon the countenance of Obadiah; but my curiosity, however, was not to be gratified, for, judging by his appearance, his thoughts were of too serious a nature to admit of laughter. I was glad when breakfast was over, and I am certain that Obadiah was more than glad.

My aunt, like most of the farmers' wives in the vicinity, had no assistance in performing her household work, except in very busy seasons. I begged of her to allow me to assist her, although I feared that I should appear very awkward in the performance of duties to which I was so little accustomed. My aunt at first refused, saying I was not accustomed to kitchen-work. But when I begged to be allowed to try my hand in assisting her, she brought me one of her large, checked aprons, which she advised me to put on. Thus attired, I washed and wiped the breakfast dishes, and arranged them in her spotless cupboard, saying to her that, while I remained an inmate of her house, she must allow me to assist her to the best of my ability, adding that I should be much happier if allowed to assist in her labors, than otherwise. Seeing me so anxious, my aunt allowed me to take my own way in the matter. I succeeded much better than I had feared; and when the morning's work was finished, my aunt laughingly said that, with a little practice, she thought I should make a very useful kitchen-maid.

In the afternoon she invited me to accompany her to the room which had been her daughter's. The room was tastefully, though not richly, furnished.

"This," said my aunt, "was Caroline's room from her childhood. I have never allowed anything to be disturbed in the room since her death, except that I occasionally air and dust it. I suppose I am somewhat childish and fanciful; but it would pain me to see this room occupied by another."

Over the mantel-piece—for almost every room in my uncle's house contained a fire-place—there hung a picture of my cousin Caroline, taken six months previous to her death. I drew nigh to look at the picture. One glance told me that she had indeed been a beautiful child. The picture was enclosed in a beautiful frame of leather-work, which had been the work of her own hands. I gazed long upon the fair picture, fondly hoping that the loss her friends had sustained, by her death, was her eternal gain, by being thus early removed from a world of sin and sorrow to her home in Heaven. Opening a drawer in a small bureau, my aunt told me to look at her school-books. By examining the books I was convinced that she must have been a child of no ordinary capacity, for her age. I also examined some of her apparel, with many other articles, which had been presents to her from friends. Seeing the tears, which I found it impossible to repress, my aunt became so much affected that I made some pretext for hastening our departure from the room; and, when we went down stairs, I endeavored to turn our conversation to some cheerful subject. to divert her mind from her sorrow, which had been so vividly recalled by our visit to that lonely room.

The view which my uncle's residence afforded of the surrounding country was very pleasing to the beholder. Whatever way the eye turned, it rested upon well-cultivated farms, on which were erected comfortable and, in many in stances, handsome and commodious dwellings. In the distance, the summits of the White Mountains were distinctly visible, they being about twenty miles distant from my uncle's residence.

Mr. and Mrs. Egmont, according to promise, paid us a visit before leaving Littleton. My uncle and aunt were much pleased by their friendly and social manner; and, when they took their leave, we parted from them with sincere regret. They left Littleton soon after, on their homeward journey.

Three weeks had now passed since my arrival at my uncle's home, and I found myself daily becoming more and more attached to my kind uncle and aunt. Obadiah appeared to feel much more at his ease in my presence than at the first. When I learned that he was an orphan-boy and had no home, I felt a deep sympathy for him; but still, when I encountered one of those glances, I often found it very difficult to avoid laughter. I learned from my aunt that he, being left an orphan, had been put to work at a very early age; and, consequently, had had but few advantages for study and improvement. He could read tolerably, and write a little. My aunt was of the opinion that, notwithstanding his peculiarities, he was possessed of good common sense, and would make good progress in study if he had any one to render him the necessary assistance. I at once offered to assist him in his studies, and proposed to him that he should spend a portion of the long evenings in study. He seemed at the first to be somewhat startled by my proposition; but, seeing that I was in earnest, gladly consented, and forthwith commenced his studies. My aunt cautioned me about laughing, if he should chance to make comical blunders; and it was well that she did so, for some of his blunders were laughable in the extreme; but "forewarned is forearmed." After a time I learned that he really possessed an intellect of no mean order. He soon made rapid progress in study. He seemed fully to appreciate the pains I took in teaching him, and endeavored, by many little acts of kindness, to show his gratitude to me.

Soon after my arrival, my aunt, one day, said to me,—

"I hope you will feel happy with us, for I wish you to consider our house as your home for the future. You know not," she continued, "how glad I am of your company, and how your presence cheers us; and we will gladly adopt you as our daughter, if you can be happy with us."

I thanked her with tears in my eyes, and added

that I was very happy in receiving so warm a welcome to their home, and would gladly do my utmost to fill a daughter's place to them. I further informed my aunt that I should be very happy to consider her house as my home, but that I should prefer teaching, as soon as I could find a desirable situation, as such had been my intention when I left Philadelphia. But when I mentioned the subject to my uncle, he seemed much hurt that I should think of such a thing. I told him that the wish to teach did not proceed from any feeling of discontent in my home, but that I thought it wrong to remain idle, while possessing an education which qualified me for usefulness. He replied that, if I felt anxious to teach, we would talk about it the following spring; but, said he, you must think no more about it for this winter, at any rate; and so the subject was suffered to drop.

We led a very quiet life at my uncle's that winter. We saw but little company, except that occasionally the wife of some neighboring farmer would drop in to take a social cup of tea with my aunt.

There was a maiden lady residing in the village of Littleton who was always a welcome visitor at my uncle's residence,—her name was Miss Priscilla Simmonds. She was somewhat advanced in years, and of a very mild and prepossessing appearance. Upon the death of her parents, which took place many years before, she was left the owner and sole tenant of the house in which she lived. She lived entirely alone, and was considered a very valuable person in the village. She seemed, upon all occasions, to adapt herself readily to surrounding circumstances. At merry-makings, no one was so lively or social as Miss Simmonds; in the chamber of sickness, no hand so gentle and no step so light as her's; and when death visited a household, her services were indispensible. Although occupying a humble position in life, she was very much respected by all who knew her. Very few there were in the vicinity but could recall some act of kindness from Miss Simmonds, rendered either to themselves or their friends; and many there were who could remember the time when her hands had prepared the form of some loved relative for its last resting-place in the grave. Thus was Miss Simmonds bound to the hearts of the people of Littleton, as by a strong cord. In person, she was tall; she had fine dark eyes, and her hair was lightly sprinkled with grey. From the expression which her countenance wore at times, I gathered the idea that she had, at some period of her life, experienced some deep sorrow. I one day enquired of my aunt if such were not the case. She gave me an evasive reply, and, perceiving that she wished to avoid the subject, I made no further enquiries.

I trust the reader will pardon this digression from my story.

In the course of the winter my uncle gave a party, to afford me an opportunity of becoming acquainted with the young people of the place. If the party lacked some of the forms and ceremonies practised in the city drawing-rooms upon like occasions, it certainly was not wanting in real enjoyment.

CHAPTER XIV.

SCHOOL AT MILL TOWN.

I BELIEVE there is no season more favorable to sober reflection that when we find ourselves alone, after mingling for a time in a scene of mirth and gaiety. After the departure of our guests, and my uncle and aunt had retired to rest, I indulged in a long fit of musing, as I sat alone by the kitchen-fire. In the silence and loneliness of the hour, my thoughts turned to my former home, and to the circumstances which had caused me to leave it; and, although I had resolved to think no more of Willie Leighton, somehow or other, on this occasion, I found my thoughts wandering to him and to the seeming fatality which had separated us. The only living relatives of whom I had any knowledge were my uncle and aunt, and the before-mentioned aunt of my mother. But a circumstance which I had heard my father mention in my childhood had of late often recurred to my mind. I recollected often hearing my father speak of a twin-brother, and that they had been left orphans at the age of eight years; also, that he, my father, had been adopted by a gentleman residing about fifty miles from the city of Philadelphia, who had given him a very good business education, and had procured for him a situation in the city when he became of suitable age. But the case had been different with his brother Charles. He too had been adopted, but by a very different kind of man from the one who had received my father. He did not give him sufficient education to qualify him for mercantile business, and at the time that Mr. Williams procured a situation for my father in the city, his brother Charles was apprenticed to learn the art of printing. He had, it seemed, entertained a dislike to the employment from the first, which increased to such a degree that he ran away from his employer; and, instead of returning to his former home, he left the city. He was then fifteen years of age. My father had never been able to gain any tidings from him, and at length came to the conclusion that he must be dead. I know not why it was, but of late this circumstance had haunted my mind continually. The idea seemed to fix itself in my mind that I should yet see this long-lost uncle. I tried to banish the thought as an absurdity, but was unable to do so. As the idea returned to my mind with such frequency, I ceased trying to banish it, and prayed that what I now thought to be an idle fancy might prove a happy reality.

How cheering to us is the return of spring, after the deep snows and severe frosts of winter.

I very much enjoyed the sugar-making season at my uncle's farm. I derived all the more pleasure from its being to me such a novelty.

Although quite happy in my uncle's home, I still wished to carry out my former design of teaching, and, as the season advanced, I again spoke to my uncle and aunt upon the subject. They were at first very unwilling to yield their consent; but, as they perceived that I was really anxious about the matter, they yielded their assent to my wishes.

About five miles west of my uncle's farm was the small village of Mill Town, so called from the number of different mills erected on the fine water-privilege it contained. As the village was small, it contained but two schools; one a public school and the other a select school, which had for three years been taught by a young lady from the State of Maine, who had relatives residing at Mill Town. But Miss Landon, for such was the lady's name, intended returning to her home in Maine in the month of June. I had formed a very pleasant acquaintance with this young lady during the winter, and she strongly advised me to secure her pupils, if I wished to teach, promising to use her influence to aid me in obtaining pupils; and, owing to her kindness, I had no difficulty in obtaining a sufficient number of pupils for opening a school. I was very glad to obtain a situation so near to my home, that I might be able to visit my uncle and aunt at least once every week, and spend my Sabbaths with them.

"After all," said my uncle, "I don't know but you are right in wishing to teach, and, I dare say, will be happier thus employed than otherwise."

Accordingly, I opened my school, about the middle of June, with twenty-five pupils. I had made arrangements to board in the house of the minister, who resided in the village. His name was Mr. Northwood, or Parson Northwood, as he was usually called by the villagers. He was very much respected on account of his many excellent qualities, both as pastor and friend. His family consisted of himself, his wife, and two little girls, who attended my school.

I was highly pleased with my school at Mill Town. My pupils were mostly girls between the ages of ten and fifteen years. I had one class of quite young boys, whose parents preferred a select to a public school.

Many years have passed since I was wont to summon those loved pupils around me in that little school-room. Since that period, when far removed from those scenes, and surrounded by circumstances widely different, memory oft recalled those pupils in that New England village.

About this time I received a letter from Aunt Patience. The letter informed me that her health was somewhat impaired, and that she sensibly felt the approaching infirmities of age. I knew not her exact age, but I was certain that she must be considerably advanced in years. She stated that she was quite happy in her home, but added,—

"My dear Clara, I had thought to have ended my days with your dear mother; and when the thought comes home to my mind, that she is now no more, it makes me very sad."

I was happy to know that, owing to the provision made for her, Aunt Patience enjoyed all the comforts of life. Since her removal to Massachusetts we had not often corresponded; but, as often as I did write, I enclosed a small sum from my own earnings, lest the interest of the deposit should prove insufficient for all her wants.

My mother left with me the injunction that, should my own life be spared, never to forget Aunt Patience in her old age; and I would cheerfully have endured any privation myself, if, by so doing, I could have added to her happiness; for the injunction of my dying mother I regarded as most sacred.

I closed my school for the summer holidays, and I was, as well as my pupils, glad to be released from the school-room during the sultry weather which prevails in the month of August.

CHAPTER XV.

A HAPPY RE-UNION.

UPON my return home, my uncle said he thought I should enjoy a change of air and scene for a time, as he fancied I was looking pale and thin. I replied that I felt quite well, and felt no wish to leave my home during vacation.

However, about this time, a party was formed among my acquaintances for visiting the White Mountains, and they were anxious that I should make one of their number; and, as my uncle and aunt strongly advised me to go, I at length consented.

The sublime scenery of the White Mountains has been so often and so ably described by tourists, that any description from me would be superfluous. Upon our arrival at the Profile House, we found it so much crowded with guests that we had no little difficulty in obtaining accommodations. When one party left, the vacancy was almost immediately filled by fresh arrivals of pleasure-seekers. Every one seemed highly to enjoy themselves, and time passed swiftly away.

I was one evening seated on the piazza, engaged in a very pleasant conversation with several ladies and gentlemen, who, like me, had sought the piazza to enjoy the refreshing coolness of the evening air, after an intensely hot day. I noticed a carriage approaching, in which several persons were seated. I did not at first pay much attention, as the arrival of strangers was a matter of very frequent occurrence; but, as the carriage drew nigh, my attention was riveted by a lady seated therein. She made some smiling remark as one of the gentlemen stepped from the carriage and assisted her to alight. That smile was sufficient—it was the very smile of Miss Edmonds, the same happy smile which had so pleased my fancy years ago. The seven years which had passed since I had seen her had somewhat changed her countenance; but her smile was the same. As she took the arm of the gentleman who accompanied her, and ascended the steps of the piazza, I stepped forward and spoke to her as any stranger might accost another in a place of public resort. I wished to see if she would recognize me. She replied to me only as she might have done to any other stranger, but without the least sign of recognition. Perceiving that she did not recognize me, I went near to her and said,—

"Can it be possible, Miss Edmonds, that you have forgotten your old pupil, Clara Roscom?"

In a moment I was clasped in her arms and felt her kisses upon my cheek. Turning to the gentleman whose arm she had left, she said,—

"Allow me, Miss Roscom, to introduce to you Mr. Harringford, my husband."

I acknowledged the introduction as well as my feelings of joyful excitement would admit of, for I knew of no other friend whose presence would afford me so much happiness as she with whom I had so unexpectedly met. Seeing that she looked very much fatigued, I conducted her at once to my own apartment. She was very anxious to learn all that had befallen me since we parted in Philadelphia; but I insisted upon her resting before entering upon the long conversation which we anticipated enjoying together.

When Miss Edmonds, or Mrs. Harringford, as I must now call her, had somewhat recovered from her fatigue, we derived mutual satisfaction from a long and confidential conversation. In giving me a brief sketch of her life during the time we had been separated, Mrs. Harringford said,—

"On going to New York, I obtained a situation as governess, which for various reasons, I did not like, and I decided upon seeking another situation. I chanced about this time to meet with a lady whose home was in South Carolina. Her husband had business which required his presence in the city of New York, and he had prevailed upon her to accompany him. The lady had, some years before, formed a slight acquaintance with Mrs. Leonard, the lady in whose house I was employed as governess, and when she visited the city she sought out Mrs. Leonard, and their former acquaintance was resumed. During one of her visits I happened to hear her remark that a friend of hers, residing in Greenville, S. C., had commissioned her if possible to find her a governess for her three little daughters, who would be willing to remain for some years; and the salary she offered was very liberal. Instantly my resolution to go South was taken. As I had anticipated, I had some difficulty in obtaining the consent of my parents to my undertaking; but, when they found that my heart was really set on going, they at length consented. I felt no fears regarding the journey, as I was to accompany Mr. and Mrs. Carlton on their homeward journey; and they promised to see me safely at my new home. It is needless for me to dwell upon particulars. I spent more than four years in the family of Mr. Leslie, where I went as governess. I was kindly treated by them, and shall ever remember them with gratitude. During the last six months of my residence with the Leslies, I became acquainted with Mr. Harringford, who is now my husband. He was transacting some business in Greenville, which detained him for a considerable time. I often met him at parties. We were mutually pleased with each other, and, when he left Greenville I was his promised wife. My home is now at Jackson, in Tennessee, where Mr. Harringford resided previous to our marriage.

"I felt a strong desire to visit my parents, at New York, this summer; and, as Mr. Harringford had heard much of the beautiful scenery of the White Mountains, he persuaded me to accompany him to New Hampshire for the purpose of visiting them, and to that circumstance I owe the happiness of again meeting with you. I have ever remembered you as the bashful school girl I left in Philadelphia, and when I found you so much changed you cannot wonder that I failed to recognize you."

In my turn I narrated to Mrs. Harringford the events of my life since we parted. Her tears flowed often as she listened to the particulars of my mother's death, for she had much loved my mother. I kept nothing back, not even the circumstance which had caused me to leave Mrs. Leighton. The intimate friendship existing between us made it easy for me to speak freely to Mrs. Harringford. She informed me that she intended visiting Philadelphia before returning South, as she had many old friends residing there. As she contemplated visiting the Leightons, I exacted from her a promise that she would conceal from them her knowledge of my residence. I had never once heard from them since leaving Philadelphia.

Mrs. Burnside was the only one with whom I had corresponded; and I had requested her to avoid mentioning the Leightons in her letters to me. But of late I had felt a strong desire to hear from them, and I requested Mrs. Harringford to give me some account of the family in the letter she proposed writing from Philadelphia.

The party of young friends who had accompanied me from Littleton were quite ready to return at the expiration of a week; but Mrs. Harringford intended remaining a week longer, and she was very anxious that I should remain with her. I therefore allowed my friends to return without me. I wished to enjoy the society of Mrs. Harringford as long as possible, for I thought it quite probable that we might never meet again.

We spent a happy week together after the return of my friends to Littleton. The only shadow upon our happiness was the thought—how soon we must be parted, perhaps for life. From all I observed of

Mr. Harringford I thought him to be worthy, in every respect, of the bride he had won.

Happy days pass swiftly by, and the morning soon arrived when we must bid each other adieu. Before we parted, Mrs. Harringford drew a costly diamond ring from her finger, and, placing it upon mine, said,—

"Wear this, my dear Clara, for my sake; and, when you look upon it, think of me, who will often think of you, and will pray for your happiness both here and hereafter."

The moment of parting had arrived. We parted on the piazza of the Profile House; they to proceed on their journey, and I to return to my uncle and aunt.

I have never since met with Mrs. Harringford. The ring she gave me at parting still encircles my finger, and, when I gaze upon it I often think of the loved friend who placed it there.

I received an affectionate welcome from my uncle and aunt upon my return, and I was truly glad to find myself once more at home. Mrs. Harringford had promised to take an early opportunity of writing to me, and I had requested her to give me some account of the Leightons. Separate from other causes, I felt anxious to hear from Birdie and Lewis, for I was strongly attached to those two affectionate children. A letter from her arrived in due time. After giving me information of many of my former friends, she said,—

"And now, Clara, it only remains for me to give you an account of my visit to Mrs. Leighton, although I fear I shall give you pain instead of pleasure by so doing. When I called on Mrs. Leighton, I was struck with surprise at her changed appearance. You doubtless remember, Clara, what beautiful hair Mrs. Leighton had. You will scarcely credit me when I inform you that it is now thickly sprinkled with grey. She appeared like one who struggled with some secret sorrow. An air of sadness seemed to reign in the home, where formerly all was joy and happiness. Mrs. Leighton so strongly urged us to spend the night with them that we could not refuse. Laura was absent, visiting some friends in the country. Georgania and Bertha were both absent, attending school. Lewis has not yet been sent from home, but attends school in the city. He has grown a fine, manly-looking boy. He made many enquiries of me, if I had seen or heard from you? I was sorry that I was not at liberty to tell him how lately I had seen you, for I am sure that it would have afforded him much pleasure. My enquiry for Willie caused a pained expression to cross the countenance of both Mr. and Mrs. Leighton.

Mr. Leighton replied briefly by saying, 'Willie is at present in England.' Later in the evening, when the gentlemen had gone out, Mrs. Leighton said to me,—'As you are an old friend, Mrs. Harringford, I will explain to you the cause of Willie's absence. You doubtless remember Clara Roscom, who was a former pupil of yours. After you left Philadelphia, she completed her education at a distant boarding-school, and soon after her return home I engaged her as governess in my family. We soon learned to love and respect Miss Roscom, on account of her many excellent qualities, and we treated her very kindly. She left us to attend to her mother during the illness which terminated in her death, and after that event she again returned to us. But, to tell you all in a few words, Willie fell in love with her, and asked her to become his wife. When I first learned the fact I suppose I made use of some rather strong language to Miss Roscom, so much so that she left my house that very night. She remained for a short time with a Mrs. Burnside, who resides in the city, and then left Philadelphia, and we have never since been able to gain any knowledge of her residence. If Mrs. Burnside knows anything of her she gives no information upon the subject. I have no doubt that she is governed by Miss Roscom's direction, for she possessed a proud spirit. I regret some things I said to her, but the thought of Willie, our pride, uniting himself by marriage to our governess put me almost beside myself with indignation. But Willie was so blinded by his love for her that all considerations of family or wealth were as nothing to him. When he learned that Miss Roscom had left the city, and he found himself unable to learn anything of her, he became embittered towards us all. He soon after declared his intention of returning to England; but, what grieves me most of all is, that he will hold no correspondence with us since leaving home. He has now been ten months absent. We have written to him again and again, but have received no reply.' As she concluded, Mrs. Leighton burst into a flood of tears, which, for some time, she was unable to check. You may believe me, Clara, when I tell you that you are happier today, while attending to the duties of your school, than is Mrs. Leighton, in her luxurious home."

Such was, in substance, the information which Mrs. Harringford's letter afforded me. I almost regretted having sought the information, for it made me very unhappy. It grieved me much to learn that Willie was self-exiled from his home and friends.

CHAPTER XVI.

MISS SIMMONDS' STORY.

THE fifteenth of September found me again installed in my position as teacher in my school at Mill Town. I still continued to board in the family of Parson Northwood. I retained all my former pupils, with the addition of several new ones.

Miss Simmonds had often invited me to pay her a visit in her home at Littleton, but I had as yet found no convenient opportunity for so doing. One Friday evening I decided to pay the long promised visit, and remain over the Sabbath with Miss Simmonds. She seemed very glad to see me, and gave me a friendly welcome to her humble home. But, humble as it was, it presented a picture of neatness and cozy comfort. After tea, and when her light household duties had all been carefully performed, we seated ourselves by a cheerful fire in her little sitting-room, and prepared to spend the long evening in social conversation. I had always been very fond of the company of Miss Simmonds. Her conversational powers were very good, and she was sufficiently well informed to render her a very agreeable companion. As the night closed in, one of those violent storms of wind and rain came on, which are so frequent in the Eastern States during the month of November. The beating of the storm without caused our warm and well-lighted room to seem all the more cheerful. As the evening advanced I observed that Miss Simmonds grew thoughtful; and, although she endeavored to be social, it was evident that her mind was occupied by something else than the subject of conversation. After a short silence, she addressed me suddenly, saying,—

"I feel inclined, Clara, to relate a story to you, which at least has the merit of truth; for it is a chapter from my own life."

I gladly assented to listen to her story, for, since I first met Miss Simmonds, I had entertained the idea that there was something of romance attached to her life.

"Thirty years ago," began Miss Simmonds, "I was not the faded, care-worn woman which you now see before you. I was born in this village. My parents were poor, but industrious people. They were blessed with two children, myself and a brother, who was two years younger than I; but, ere he reached the age of ten, we were called to lay him in the grave, leaving me the sole comfort and joy of my bereaved parents. They had very much loved my little brother; and, when death claimed him, all the love which he would have shared with me, had he lived, was lavished upon me. There is little in my childhood and youth worthy of notice, as we occupied an humble sphere in life. I suppose you will hardly credit me, Clara, when I teli you that, at the age of sixteen, I was called beautiful. It was something to which I had given but little thought; but the ear of youth is ever open to flattery, and I must confess that my vanity was flattered by being called beautiful by the residents of the then small village of Littleton.

"When I was about eighteen years of age," continued Miss Simmonds, "a young lawyer, by the name of Almont, opened an office in this village, for the practice of his profession. He came among us suddenly, and he informed those with whom he first made acqaintance, that he had formerly resided in Massachusetts. Many wondered at his locating himself here, as the village was then but small, and offered few inducements to professional men. He was very affable and pleasing in his address, and soon made the acquaintance of many of the young people of the village; and we soon found him to be a very agreeable addition to our pic-nic excursions and other parties for pleasure and amusement. He paid marked attention to me from the time when we first became acquainted; and, to shorten my story, after an acquaintance of six months, he asked me to become his wife. I am now an old woman, Clara, and need not blush to tell you that I had learned to love him with a deep affection, and I yielded a willing assent, provided that my parents approved. True, I had no knowledge of his connections or former life; but, since his residence in our village, his conduct had been irreproachable, and he was fast gaining the respect and confidence of all who knew him. There was something very attractive in his personal appearance; he seemed to have seen much of the world, for so young a man, for he spoke in a familiar manner of many distant scenes and places. When he sought my hand in marriage, my parents did not object. He was gaining quite a lucrative practice both in Littleton and adjacent places, and he declared his intention of making Littleton his permanent home. Doubtless, this influenced my parents to favor his suit, as the thought of my settling in my native village was very pleasing to them. He was very much flattered by society, and I was all the more pleased to find myself the object of his choice. When our engagement became known, I had good reason for believing myself to be envied by many of my female acquaintances

Neither they nor I were aware how soon their envy was to be turned to pity. An early day was appointed for our marriage, and my poor parents exerted themselves to give me a suitable wedding outfit. About this time, Mr. Almont had business which obliged him to leave Littleton for a short time. When he bade me adieu I felt a foreboding of evil; and, after he had gone, I experienced a depression of spirits, for which I could not account. But, when he had been a week absent, and I received from him a cheerful letter, informing me of his return in a few days, I strove to banish my sad thoughts and busied myself in preparing my wedding outfit. Going one day to the Post Office, with the expectation of finding there a letter from Mr. Almont, I received this instead."

As she spoke, Miss Simmonds unfolded a letter, which I had observed her take from a drawer before commencing her story. It read thus:—

"BOSTON, June 4th, 18—.

"To Miss Priscilla Simmonds:

"Although you are, personally, a stranger to me, I nevertheless take the liberty of addressing you. By the merest chance I learned your name and residence, also, that you are shortly to be united in marriage to Mr. George Almont, a lawyer from the city of Boston.

"I feel it an imperative duty, before that event shall take place, to inform you that I am the wedded wife of the same George Almont, whom you are about to marry. He came to Boston about five years since, having, as he said, just completed his studies in the city of New York. He opened an office in this city for the practice of his profession; and, as his external appearance was pleasing, he soon gained an entrance into good society. I need not inform you that he was likely to make a favorable impression upon the mind of a young lady just entering society. He rose rapidly in his profession; and, although my parents were wealthy, when they saw how deeply I was attached to him, they did not object to my receiving his addresses, as he bid fair to rise to a position of wealth and influence. It is needless, as well as painful, for me to dwell upon the subject. Two years after he first came to Boston we were married. We soon removed to our own dwelling, which was a wedding gift to me, from my father. For a time he treated me with the utmost kindness and affection. But you may believe me, Miss Simmonds, when I inform you that he has been a dissipated, unprincipled man from his youth. His seemingly correct habits had merely been put on, for the purpose of gaining him an entrance into respectable society. When he began to treat me with indifference and neglect, for a long time I bore it in silence; but I was at length forced to acquaint my parents of the matter. My father soon took measures to ascertain what manner of life he had led while pursuing his studies in New York; and the information he gained was very discreditable to Mr. Almont. But my parents advised me, as we were married, to try if, by kindness, I could not reclaim him from his evil ways. I willingly followed their advice, for I still loved him; but, I suppose the restraint which for a time he had imposed upon himself made him all the more reckless when he returned to his evil courses. He soon seemed to lose all respect for me as well as for himself; and his conduct became so vicious that my father recalled me to his home, and forbade Mr. Almont from ever again entering his dwelling. I could, I presume, have obtained a divorce from him with little difficulty, but I shrank from the publicity attached to such a course. I still reside with my father and mother. Mr. Almont left Boston soon after I returned to my parents. We heard nothing of him for some time; but we lately heard from a reliable source that he was residing in Littleton, in New Hampshire, and also of his approaching marriage. Nothing but a sense of duty would have induced me to make this communition to you. I would save another young life from being shadowed by the same cloud which has darkened mine. Should you doubt the truth of what I have written, you can easily satisfy yourself, by either visiting this city in person, or causing any of your relatives so to do. Enclosed you will find the street and number of my residence. I sincerely hope you will receive this communication in the spirit with which it is written, and that is, one of kindness, and a desire to save you from the sorrows which I have experienced.

"Yours truly,

"MALVINA ALMONT."

Miss Simmonds continued,—

"You may be able to imagine, but I cannot describe the effect produced upon my mind by the perusal of this letter. I felt stupefied and bewildered. How I reached my home I could never tell. I entered the house just as my father and mother were sitting down to their noon-day meal. As soon as my mother caught sight of me she enquired of me what was the matter? I suppose the agony of my mind was depicted upon my countenance. Without a word, I placed the letter in her hand, which, after perusing, she handed to my father. The natural temper of my father was rash and impulsive, and the contents of that letter exasperated him beyond control. He used many bitter words, and threatened dire vengeance upon young Almont, should he ever again enter our dwelling. My mother begged of him to desist, saying that if he were indeed guilty, as the letter proved him to be, his sin would certainly bring its own punishment. When we had succeeded in quieting the anger of my father, we were able to converse upon the matter in a calm and rational manner. We finally decided that my father should read the letter to Mr. Almont upon his return, and see what effect it would produce upon him. Three days later he came. He entered our dwelling and accosted us with his usual bland and smiling manner. In a short time, my father turned and said,—'During your absence, Mr. Almont, my daughter has received a most unaccountable letter which I wish to read to you, hoping you may be able to explain it.' The paleness which overspread his countenance on hearing my father's words put to flight the hope I had cherished that he would be able to prove the letter a falsehood. Without any further remark, my father read the letter to him, word for word. As he concluded he said,—'And now, Mr. Almont, unless you are prepared to prove the information contained in this letter to be untrue,

I wish you immediately to leave my dwelling; and, if you take my advice, you will also leave this village, for I cannot abide the sight of a wretch such as this letter proves you to be; and your silence bears testimony to its truth. Begone! I say, from the humble, but, heretofore, happy home, which your baseness has darkened by sorrow.' As my father uttered these words, he stamped with his foot, and pointed to the door. Without a word, Mr. Almont left the house; and, on the day following, we learned that he had left Littleton, and gone, no one knew whither. Many surmises arose concerning his sudden departure, for it was well known that we were engaged to be married; but no one had any knowledge of the facts of the matter. When the wonder had subsided, which any unusual event occasions in a small village, the subject was suffered to rest. I felt stricken as by a sudden blow. I felt no interest in life; but I endeavored, when in the presence of my parents, to assume a cheerfulness which was far from being the real state of my mind.

"To a few old and tried friends only did we make known the real truth of the circumstances attending the departure of Mr. Almont from Littleton. Time passed on. Those who knew my sorrows respected them, and the name of George Almont ceased to be mentioned among our acquaintances. But it was something which I could never cease to remember. I had loved George Almont as one of my nature can love but once in her life; and, when I learned that I had been deceived in regard to his true character, the knowledge was very bitter to me. I loved him still—not as he really was, but I still loved the memory of what I had supposed him to be, when I gave him my affection. There are few lessons in life more bitter to either man or woman than to find themselves deceived by one to whom they have given their best affections. For a time I yielded to a bitter and desponding spirit. I excluded myself from all society, and brooded in solitude over my sorrow. I so far yielded to this unhealthy tone of mind that I gave up attending church, and I caused my parents much grief and anxiety by the sullen and apathetic state of mind in which I indulged.

"During the winter which succeeded the events of which I have spoken, there were a series of special meetings held in the Congregational Church in this village. A general interest was manifested in the subject of religion by both old and young. Many of those who had been my former companions were hopefully converted. I had formerly been of a gay and lively disposition, fond of dress and amusement. The subject of religion was one to which I had scarcely ever given a thought. The world and its pleasures occupied my whole heart; and, when the world disappointed me, I knew not where to turn for comfort. True, I had, from a child, attended to the outward forms of religion, but my heart was untouched; and I now see that it required a great earthly sorrow to turn my thoughts heavenward. I at first refused to attend the meetings of which I have spoken, though often strongly urged to do so; but, one evening, my parents so strongly urged me to accompany them to hear an aged minister from another State that I at length consented to go. It is a matter of thankfulness to me this day that I attended that meeting. As I have said, the minister was an old man; his hair was white as snow. There was something remarkably pleasant and venerable in his appearance. No one who heard his voice and gazed upon his mild countenance, could doubt that they listened to a good man. During the first prayer, on that evening, my heart became softened and subdued; and, when he gave out his text, from Matthew xi. chap., 28, and two following verses, I listened to him with rapt attention. It seemed almost that he understood my individual case. In the course of his sermon, he said:—'I presume there are few in this congregation who have not some burden of sorrow which they would gladly have removed.

Shall I tell you how you may be released from this burden? Kneel humbly at the foot of the Cross; and, while you pray for the forgiveness of your past sins, make a firm resolve, in the strength of the Lord, that your future life shall be given to His service; if you do this with sincerity, you shall surely find rest unto your souls. You need have no fears that you will be rejected, for hath not the Saviour said:—Him that cometh unto me I will in no wise cast out. You may, this very night, exchange your burden of sin and sorrow for the yoke which is easy and the burden which is light.'

"I have," said Miss Simmonds, "a distinct recollection of the look and manner of that aged man as he uttered these words, and it is a matter of heartfelt thankfulness to me this day that ever I heard his voice; for he it was who first guided my wandering feet into the paths of peace. When I returned to my home the words of that good man followed me. I thought much on the words of his text. Surely, thought I, if all are invited to come to the Saviour, I must be included in the number. Why may I not go now? With these thoughts in my mind, I kneeled in prayer. I prayed earnestly for the pardon of my sins, and resolved, from that moment, to begin a new life. Before rising from my knees I experienced a sense of pardoning love, and I was happy.

"It was now that I became sensible of the wrong I had been guilty of, in allowing my sorrow to cause me to neglect my duties, for there is no one in any station of life but has claims of duty. I again engaged actively in the duties of life, with a feeling of thankfulness that I was privileged to cheer the declining years of my parents. Year after year passed away. I still remained with my father and mother; and I felt no wish to leave them, although I had more than one opportunity for so doing. My mother died at the age of sixty-five. I nursed her tenderly through a long and painful illness, and closed her eyes in death. My father and I were now left alone in our home. He was several years older than my mother. The infirmities of age were coming fast upon him.

CHAPTER XVII.

PENITENT, AND FORGIVEN.

ON a stormy evening, like this, we were sitting together in this room, when our attention was arrested by a timid knock at the door. My father opened the door, and I heard some one, in a feeble voice, ask permission to enter the house. My father conducted the stranger in, and gave him a seat by our cheerful fire. When the stranger entered the room, and I gained a view of his face, I at once knew that I stood face to face with George Almont. When I suddenly pronounced his name, my father made a hasty movement as if to speak with anger, but I gave him an imploring look, and he remained silent. Although greatly changed, it was, nevertheless, George Almont who was now in our presence. After a few moments of silence; for, after my exclamatory utterance of his name, neither of us had spoken, he turned his eyes, in which the light of disease painfully burned, and said,—'You do well not to reproach me; the time for that is past, for I am, as you may see, on the verge of the grave. I have striven with disease, that I might reach this place, and, if possible, obtain your forgiveness 'ere my eyes shall close in death. I know I have darkened a life, which, but for me, might have been bright and joyous. It is too much for me to expect your forgiveness, yet I would hear you pronounce that blessed word before I die. You may *now* believe me when I say, that it was my love for you which led me to deceive you. Knowing my wife's dread of any publicity being attached to her name, I thought the knowledge that I had a living wife would never reach you. Of the sinfulness of my conduct I did not at that time pause to think. I now sincerely thank my wife for preventing a marriage which, in the sight of God, must have been but mockery. I now speak truly when I say to you, I never loved my wife; I married her for money. As I had no affection for her, my former habits of dissipation soon regained their hold on me. It will afford me some comfort to know that I have made strictly true confession to you. I have not, to my knowledge, a living relation in the wide world; and, till I met with you, I knew not the meaning of the word love; and I still believe that, had I met you earlier in life, your influence would have caused me to become a useful man, and an ornament to my profession. But it is useless to talk now of what cannot be recalled. When I left this village, years ago, I was equally indifferent as to whither I went or what I did. I felt no wish to return to my wife; and, had I been thus inclined, I well knew the just contempt and scorn I should meet with, although I believe she had once loved me. But I knew them to be a proud family, and I felt certain they would never overlook the disgrace and sorrow I had brought upon them. I have never since seen my wife, but I lately learned that she, with the rest of the family, removed to a western city some years ago. Since leaving this place I have wandered far and wide, never remaining long in one place. My mind has never been at rest, and, for that reason, I have been a lonely wanderer all these years. But my dissipated habits have done their work, and I feel that my earthly course is well nigh ended. I have dragged my feeble body to your dwelling, with the hope of obtaining your forgiveness 'ere I am summoned into eternity.'

"While listening to him, I had seated myself at my father's side. As he concluded, I said to my father, in a low voice,—'If we forgive not our fellow-mortal, how can we expect the forgiveness of our Heavenly Father for our many sins?' I rose from my seat and extending to him my hand, said,—'You have, Mr. Almont, my entire forgiveness for all the sorrow you have caused me, and I hope you will also obtain the forgiveness of God.' My father also came forward, and, taking his hand, granted him his forgiveness. When he finished speaking he seemed entirely exhausted. My father led him into the adjoining room, and assisted him to lie down upon his own bed. He also gave him a little wine, which seemed somewhat to revive him. Observing that he rapidly grew worse, my father summoned our physician, who was an old friend, and knew all the circumstances connected with our former acquaintance with Mr. Almont. When the physician arrived, he expressed the opinion that death was fast approaching; said he,—'I do not think he will see another sun rise,'—and he did not. He said but little, and suffered but little pain; but he sank rapidly. His mind was clear to the last. A short time before his death, he turned his eyes, over which the film of death was gathering, to my father, and, with much difficulty, said,—'Pray—for—me.' My father knelt and implored the mercy of heaven on the soul that was departing. I could not bear that he should leave the world without one word in regard to what were his feelings in the near prospect of death. Going near, I said,—'Do you feel willing to trust yourself to the Saviour's mercy to penitent sinners?' He gave a sign of assent, and a more peaceful expression settled on his countenance. 'I know,' said he, in a whisper, 'that I have been a grievous sinner for many long years, yet the forgiveness guaranteed by you, whom I have so deeply injured, gives me a hope that God will also forgive the sins, for which I now trust I feel deeply penitent.' After this, he lay for a short time in a kind of stupor. Suddenly, he opened his eyes, and they rested upon my father, who stood by his bed-side. His lips moved slightly, and my father distinguished the words,—'Pray for me.' He again knelt and prayed earnestly, in subdued voice, for the spirit that was then entering the unknown future. A few moments after, and the soul of George Almont was summoned to leave its earthly tenement. When the small procession that had followed his remains to their last resting-place turned from the new-made grave, the two following lines from Gray's Elegy came unbidden to my mind:—

> 'No further seek his merits to disclose,
> Or draw his frailties from their dread abode.'

"Perhaps, Clara," continued Miss Simmonds, "you may, in your walks through what is now called 'The Old Burial-ground,' a short distance from the village, have observed a lonely-looking grave, marked by a plain marble head-stone, and shaded by the branches of an aged tree; you may have noticed this grave, and never given a thought to the poor mortal who sleeps there. That is the grave of George Almont. Three years later, my father died, and I was left alone. Since that period I have lived sometimes alone, and occasionally spending a short time with any family who happen to require my services, as I find it necessary to do something for my own support. I have been able to support myself in comfort and respectability, and, even occasionally, to bestow charity in a small way to those less favored than myself. I know not why I felt so much inclined to relate these circumstances to you this evening, for you are the first stranger to whom I ever related the story connected with my early life. I am no longer young, but the memory of my early sorrows time can never efface; although, aided by religion, I have learned resignation and cheerfulness. One thing more," continued Miss Simmonds, "and I have done."

Rising, she opened a drawer and, taking a locket therefrom, she placed it in my hand, saying,—

"You may, if you wish, Clara, look upon a picture of George Almont, taken when he was twenty-five years of age."

Opening the locket, I looked upon the picture of what must have been a very fine-looking young man. I never beheld a more prepossessing countenance. No one who looked upon that picture would have dreamed of the sad story attached to the life of the original. Closing the locket, I gave it back to Miss Simmonds, who replaced it in the drawer without once looking upon the picture it contained. In conclusion, Miss Simmonds said,—

"I hope you are not wearied with an old woman's story."

I assured her that it had deeply interested me, although I feared the recital had been painful to her.

CHAPTER XVIII.

A NEW JOY.

I RETURNED to my school, after having enjoyed a very pleasant visit with Miss Simmonds. I thought much of the story she had related to me. I endeavored to learn a useful lesson from the cheerful resignation which Miss Simmonds evinced by her daily life.

Obadiah still pursued his studies with much zeal; and, upon my return home, each succeeding week, I gave him all the assistance in my power. The amount of knowledge he had derived, by devoting his leisure hours to study, was indeed wonderful. Awkward as he at first appeared to me, I found, as he progressed in his studies, that he possessed a powerful intellect, which only required proper culture to enable him to become a talented and useful man.

I now pass, with a few words, over a period of two years. During all this time I had continued the labors of my school at Mill Town, still considering my uncle's house as my home. Obadiah had, by the advice of my uncle, gone to pursue his studies in Massachusetts, having decided to obtain a thorough education. He intended fitting himself for college, and had saved money sufficient to defray his expenses while so doing. Miss Simmonds still resided in her home at Littleton, and the longer I enjoyed her friendship the more did I love and respect her. I had received several letters from Aunt Patience during the past two years. She had repeatedly urged me to visit her, but, for various reasons, I had been unable to do so; but, at this time, I determined to pay her a visit. Accordingly, I prepared for my journey to Woodville, a small village in Massachusetts, where she resided. She was very much pleased to see me. She was much changed since I had last seen her. Her once vigorous and active form was beginning to bow beneath the weight of years. She seemed to be very comfortably situated with her relatives; for, having but a small family, they were able to give her a quiet home. I enquired of her if she felt happy in her home?

"I feel quite happy and contented," she replied, "and have no wish to leave my present home, till you marry and possess a home of your own, when I should be very glad to make my home with you."

I replied that I had no intention of marrying at present; but, that if that event should take place during her lifetime, I should be most happy to receive her into my home.

The village of Woodville was not large; but its location was romantic and pleasant, being bounded on one side by a range of high hills, and on the other by a beautiful river. I was highly pleased with the place, and with the kind family with whom Aunt Patience resided. When I had spent about ten days at Woodville, I received a letter from my uncle, requesting my return home without delay. In a postscript he informed me that I need not be alarmed, as both he and my aunt were in good health; but that he did not wish to assign a reason for requesting my return. I could not imagine what had caused my uncle to summon me home, as he was aware that I had intended spending several weeks with my aunt; and I made all possible haste to set out on my homeward journey, and left Woodville the next morning after receiving my uncle's letter. When my uncle and aunt met me on my return, I knew by their manner that something unusual had taken place in my absence; but I judged from the countenance of both that, whatever the event might be, it was one of joy rather than sorrow. My uncle soon said,—

"Can you bear good news, Clara?"

I replied that I thought I could.

"Then," continued my uncle, "I have the happiness of informing you that the hopes you had so long cherished of seeing your uncle Charles will be realized, for he has arrived."

'Ere I could frame a reply, the door of the adjoining room opened, and my new-found uncle came hastily forward. He evinced much emotion as he tenderly embraced me, saying,—

"Your face strongly reminds me of the twin brother from whom I parted so many years ago. You know not how happy I am in finding the daughter of my dear brother."

I could trace in the features of my uncle Charles a resemblance to my dear father; but, as my father had died while quite a young man, the resemblance, at my uncle's time of life, was less striking than otherwise it might have been.

My uncle Charles was now sixty-five years old; but travel and exposure caused him to look much older than he really was. He informed me that he had first visited Philadelphia, with the hope of finding my father; and, when he learned that my father and mother were both dead, he next enquired if they left any children? He learned that they left one daughter, who had resided for some time in the family of the Leightons, as governess; but had left Philadelphia three years since. He next sought out the Leightons, hoping to learn my residence; but they of course could give him no information upon the subject. They directed him to Mrs. Burnside, who at first was reluctant to give the information he sought; but, when he informed her of the relationship I bore to him, she directed him to my uncle Wayland, in New Hampshire, at whose residence he arrived one week previous to my return from Massachusetts. He soon after gave us the following brief account of his life, since he left Philadelphia, when a boy, which I reserve for the succeeding chapter of my story.

CHAPTER XIX.

UNCLE CHARLES.

MY uncle began his story as follows:—

"When I left Philadelphia, I had no definite object in view. I left without seeing my brother, to avoid the pain of parting, for we tenderly loved each other. His disposition and mine were widely different; he was quiet, industrious, and very persevering in whatever he undertook; while I, on the other hand, was rash, impulsive, and very impatient of restraint. My adopted father apprenticed me to learn the art of printing, without in the least consulting my wishes in the matter. It seemed to me that he might have granted me the privilege of choosing my employment; and, his failing to do so, roused my indignation and doubled the dislike I already felt to the occupation of a printer. It was very hard for me to leave without seeing my brother; but I decided that, as he was very well contented in his situation, I had best go away quietly, so that, whatever might befall me, I should not be the means of bringing trouble to him. I had decided to leave my master the first opportunity that should offer for so doing. He one day gave me a sharp and, as I thought, unmerited rebuke, and ended by striking me a blow. That blow caused me to form the decision of leaving him at once, and that very night I left Philadelphia. I made my way to the city of New York, where I managed to live for a time by selling newspapers; but my profits were so small that I soon became disgusted with the employment, and I obtained the situation of waiter in a large hotel, where I remained for some time. I often thought of writing to my brother; but I was aware that the knowledge of my employment would be painful to him, for he was of a proud and sensitive nature. Time passed on, and I at length sailed as cabin-boy in a vessel bound for Liverpool, in England. I followed the sea for many years; and, in the bustle and turmoil of a sailor's life, I almost forgot my brother, from whom I had been so long separated. Yet, sometimes, in the lonely hours of my night-watch on deck, when out in mid-ocean, would my thoughts turn to that once-loved brother, and tears would dim my eyes as memory recalled the days of our early childhood.

"I rose in my profession till I arrived at the position of second mate. It was at this time that, during a stay of some weeks duration in an English port, I met with one who won my affections; and, one year after, we were married. My wife resided with her friends in England, while I continued to follow the sea. My wife was to me an object of almost idolatrous attachment. Each time I visited England, I found it the harder to bid farewell to my wife, and again embark on the ocean. We had one child, a beautiful boy. I named him Henry, after my brother. When we had been two years married, I made a voyage to the Indies, and was absent nearly two years. When I returned, I learned that my wife and child had both been for some time dead. When I learned the sad truth I was like one bereft of reason. I could not reconcile myself to the thought that, in this world, I could never again behold my beloved wife and child. The very darkness of despair settled on my mind. I had not then, as I have since done, looked heavenward for consolation amid the sorrows of life.

"I can dwell no longer upon this dark period of my life, but hasten onward to the close of my story. I continued to follow the life of a sailor for some years after my bereavement. The hurry and bustle attendant upon my calling served in some measure to drive away thoughts of the past; but, after a time, I even grew weary of the sea; and, when I heard of the famous gold regions discovered in Australia, I felt a strong desire to visit the place. The desire of making money had less to do with my decision of going there than had the wish for change and excitement of some kind. Accordingly, I abandoned my sailor life, and made my way among the hundreds who were crowding to the gold regions of Australia.

"At that time I was poor, for I had never possessed the faculty for saving money. I was unaccustomed to the labors of mining, and, in many instances, the knowing ones took me in, and for a long time I realized but little from my labors. But, as I persevered, against many discouragements, year after year, I at length began to be successful. I finally bought a claim, which, quite unexpectedly to me, yielded a golden harvest, and I soon found myself rich beyond my most sanguine expectations.

"Year after year I determined to re-visit Philadelphia; but, by this time my mind had become much engrossed by money-making, and each succeeding year brought fresh claims upon my time and attention.

"Time passed on, till I found myself fast growing old. I felt an intense longing to return to the land of my birth, and spend the few years which might remain to me of life in my native city. During my residence in Australia I met with a man who informed me that he was in Philadelphia at the time of my brother's marriage; and it was a severe trial when I found, upon my return, that my brother and his wife had both been many years dead. During my homeward journey, I had formed the decision of spending my remaining days in the home of my brother, as I wished for quiet and repose. When I learned that they were both dead, all the affection of my worn and world-weary heart turned toward their orphan daughter."

Turning to me, my uncle said,—

"Will you go, my dear child, and make bright the home of your aged uncle?"

I was about to give a joyful assent, when the thought of the kind uncle and aunt I must leave, caused me to hesitate. It seemed to me that they possessed a claim upon my affections superior to any other, and I was at a loss to decide as to what was my duty. I therefore remained silent, not knowing what reply to make. Observing my hesitation, my uncle Wayland said,—

"Lonely as we shall be without you, my dear Clara, I yet think it your duty to go with your uncle Charles, who is still more lonely than we. We must not be selfish; and I think we should feel willing to give you up."

I was much relieved to know that my uncle and aunt Wayland were willing that I should go, although

I well knew their willingness was caused by what they considered my duty to my aged relative.

Till I prepared to leave my uncle and aunt, I knew not how tenderly I had learned to love them. I resigned my school at Mill Town, with much sorrow, for I had become strongly attached to my pupils. As my uncle and aunt tenderly embraced me at parting, my uncle said, while the tears coursed down his furrowed cheeks,—

"Remember, dear Clara, there will ever be for you a daughter's welcome, both in our hearts and home."

CHAPTER XX.

LIGHTS AND SHADOWS.

I WAS agitated by many contending emotions as I alighted from the train which had borne me to Philadelphia; but, along with many sad thoughts, came the consoling one, that I had not returned to my native city the friendless being I had left it.

We stayed for a short time with my old friends, the Burnsides, while my uncle attended to the business of buying and furnishing a suitable residence.

Before removing to our home, my uncle engaged Mrs. Burnside to find a person suitable to occupy the position of housekeeper in his dwelling. It immediately occurred to Mrs. Burnside that my old friend, Mrs. O'Flaherty, would be well qualified for that position. She had remained in the service of Mrs. Wallingford since the time when I first introduced her to the reader; but, fortunately for us, Mr. Wallingford was about removing his family to a distant State, and they would no longer require her services. Mrs. O'Flaherty was overjoyed when she learned that she was to reside with me. When I, in company with Mrs. Burnside, called to make the necessary arrangements for her removal to her new home, I could hardly believe that the tidy, well-dressed matron I saw could be the same poor woman to whom I had given food when hungry and destitute.

"Indade," exclaimed Mrs. O'Flaherty, "an' I niver expected to see the happy day whin I would live wid you, in a home av yer own."

The matter was soon arranged, and an early day appointed for her to commence her duties as housekeeper in the dwelling of my uncle.

It was quite a change for me to find myself so suddenly removed from my position as teacher in a small school and installed as mistress in my uncle's elegant home in Walnut Street, Philadelphia. We found Mrs. O'Flaherty very trustworthy, and well qualified in every way for her position.

Soon after our return to Philadelphia, my uncle accompanied me to the graves of my parents. I cannot describe my feelings when I found myself after so long an absence, again standing by the spot where reposed the dust of my loved father and mother. I seemed almost to feel their presence, and the tears I shed were gentle and refreshing. Seated by those graves, I, for the first time, spoke to my uncle of the circumstances which had caused me to leave Mrs. Leighton, and remove from Philadelphia. He expressed much sympathy for me, and said,—

"You should endeavor to banish these circumstances from your mind. You are young, and, I trust, have yet many years of happy life before you."

I learned from Mrs. Burnside that Mr. Leighton had lately met with several heavy losses in business. Willie was still in England. He had written two or three letters to Birdie, but had corresponded with no other member of the family. Laura and Georgania had both married, and removed to a distant city. Birdie had finished her studies, and returned home. Lewis was attending school some two hundred miles from the city.

Mrs. Burnside further informed me that the health of Mrs. Leighton was very much impaired. According to the information I gained from Mrs. Burnside, there seemed to have been a great change in the family of Mr. Leighton since I left Philadelphia.

Time passed happily away in my new home. We often saw company, for all my old friends soon sought me out, when they learned of my return to the city; and my uncle, being of a social disposition, extended a kindly welcome to them all. Birdie Leighton called. I was truly glad to see her, and she seemed equally happy to meet me; but our meeting could not be otherwise than constrained and formal; and, owing to circumstances, anything like intimacy was, of course, out of the question. I had almost forgotten to mention that, among the first to call upon me in my new home, were Mrs. and Miss Kingsley, for she was *Miss* Kingsley still; the same who were so much shocked by meeting with a governess at a fashionable party. Surely, thought I, my uncle's money is working wonders, when I am already patronized by the exclusive Mrs. Kingsley. Their call I have never yet returned.

While walking one day, with a friend, I caught a glimpse of Mrs. Leighton, as she rode past in her carriage. She was so much changed that, at the first, I hardly recognized her; but, upon looking more closely, I saw that it was indeed Mrs. Leighton.

A year and a half had now glided by since my return to Philadelphia. Nothing worthy of note had taken place during this time.

The last letter from my friends in New Hampshire informed me that Obadiah was still pursuing his studies, with a view to the ministry. This afforded me but little surprise, as I had often heard him make remarks which led me to think he had an inclination to that calling.

One sultry evening in August, I retired early to my own room, as I was suffering from a severe headache. The usual remedies afforded me relief from pain; but I found myself unable to sleep. As the hour grew late, my nervous restlessness so much increased that, abandoning the idea of rest, I rose and lighted my lamp. I felt almost alarmed at my own agitation, which seemed so unaccountable. I seemed to feel the foreshadowing of some unusual event. After a time, I closed my window, and was about to extinguish my lamp and again seek repose, when I was startled by the sudden ringing of fire-bells. Hastily unclosing my window, I heard the sound of "Fire! fire!" echoed by many voices, and accompanied by the hasty tread of many feet upon the pavements. I observed the appearance of fire a few streets distant, but was unable to make out its exact location. I listened eagerly, hoping to gain from the many voices which reached my ears some account of the burning building. Presently the words—"Mr. Leighton's house is burning!" reached my excited ears. I saw that the fire was raging fearfully, as the adjacent streets were becoming lighter by the flames. I was about to call my uncle, when I heard his step approaching. A moment after he rapped at my door. Just then Mrs. O'Flaherty rushed up the stairs, breathless with terror.

"May the Saints defend us!" she exclaimed, as she burst into my apartment; "but is the city on fire?

For wasn't it the light o' the flames shinin' on me windy, that 'waked me out o' me sound slape."

My uncle endeavored to allay her terrors, telling her that the city was certainly not on fire, although there was a burning building in our near vicinity. He soon declared his intention of visiting the scene of the fire. I begged him to be careful and not expose himself to danger.

After my uncle left us, we stationed ourselves on the upper piazza, to watch the progress of the flames. From the confusion of voices in the street below I caught the words,—

"Poor Birdie Leighton is nowhere to be found, and it is feared she has perished in the flames."

I shuddered as I listened to these words. It was a terrible thought to me, that my once loved pupil had met with a death so dreadful. But I was unwilling to give up the hope that she would yet be, if not already, saved. We waited long in anxious suspense for the return of my uncle; but the day had begun to dawn before he came. I feared to ask what I longed to know. He must have read my anxiety in my countenance, for he soon said to me,—

"The Leightons are now all safe in the house of a neighbor; but Birdie came near meeting her death in the flames."

To my eager enquiries, he replied,—

"That before Mr. Leighton awoke, their sleeping apartment was filled with smoke, with which the flames were already beginning to mingle. He bore his wife from the apartment; and, with her in his arms, hastened to awake Birdie, whose room adjoined their own. She hastily threw on a portion of her clothing, and prepared to accompany her father and mother in their descent from the chambers. She had fainted from terror, while crossing the upper hall; and it was not till Mr. Leighton reached the open air with his wife in his arms, that he missed Birdie from his side. On leaving her apartment, he had besought her to keep close by him, as her mother required all his attention. The agony of Mr. and Mrs. Leighton, when, upon reaching the open air, they found Birdie to be not with them, may be better imagined than described. Mrs. Leighton became well-nigh frantic, and was almost forcibly conveyed to the house of a neighbor. As soon as Mr. Leighton was relieved from the care of his wife, he rushed toward the burning building, saying that he would either rescue Birdie or perish with her. But, ere he reached the entrance, a man issued from the house, bearing Birdie in his arms. The brave man had rushed up the burning staircase, and reached the spot where Birdie still lay, in a state of insensibility. Hastily enveloping her person in a thick, heavy shawl, which he had taken with him for the purpose, he rushed with her down the perilous staircase, and reached the open air in safety, his clothing only being singed by the flames. Never," said my uncle, "did I hear such a shout of joy as went up from the assembled multitude when the man who rescued Birdie came from the house, bearing her in safety to her father. Mr. Leighton fell on his knees and fervently thanked God for sparing the life of his child. 'Now,' said he, 'I am content that my dwelling should burn.' He grasped the hand of her rescuer, and said, with much emotion,—'Words are too poor to express my gratitude; but, if my life is spared, you shall be rewarded.' 'I want no reward,' said the noble man, 'for having done my duty.' He was a laboring man, and had a large family dependent upon his daily earnings. Quite a large sum of money was soon raised among the assembled crowd, which he would not accept, till compelled to do so by the thankful multitude."

In conclusion, my uncle said,—

"Consciousness returned to Birdie soon after she was conveyed into the open air, and she was speedily conveyed to her anxious mother. The rescue of Birdie from so dreadful a death was to me a matter of deep and heartfelt thankfulness."

Previous to the burning of Mr. Leighton's dwelling, his pecuniary affairs, according to common report, had become very much embarrassed ; and this event seemed the finishing stroke to his ill-fortune. They were unable to save anything from their dwelling, being thankful to escape with their lives. He still continued his business ; but, it was said, his liabilities were heavier than he was able to meet. He rented a moderate-sized house, and removed thither with his family. Those who visited them said it was but plainly furnished. Their servants, with one or two exceptions, had all been dismissed.

CHAPTER XXI.

RECONCILED.

LEWIS was recalled from school in the early autumn; and, soon after, the news of Mr. Leighton's failure was eagerly discussed in the business world.

Lewis called to see me soon after his return. He was now a manly youth of fifteen. I was much pleased to see him; and, when he rose to go, after a lengthy call, I invited him to call often upon us. My uncle took a great fancy to the boy, and many evenings found Lewis our guest. I learned from Lewis, and others, that the health of Mrs. Leighton had so much failed that she was now entirely confined to the house.

Mr. Leighton had lately written to Willie, giving him an account of their misfortunes, and of the failing health of his mother; and concluded by earnestly requesting his return home, as he feared that it was Willie's absence which was preying so heavily upon the mind of Mrs. Leighton as to cause, in a great measure, her failing health.

Lewis called one evening, and, upon entering the

parlor, handed me a note. As I glanced at my name on the envelope, I at once recognized the hand-writing of Mrs. Leighton. Hastily breaking the seal, I read the following lines :—

"ELM STREET, Nov. 25th, 18—.

"To Miss Clara Roscom :

"I am extremely anxious for an interview with you; but my state of health will not allow of my leaving my own residence. I therefore earnestly request you to accompany Lewis upon his return home, for I *must* see you. I am sensible that I have no right to ask of you this favor; but I trust that the kindness of your heart will induce you to comply with my request.

"Yours truly,

"CYNTHIA LEIGHTON."

When I had finished reading the note I could not forbear from questioning Lewis as to its meaning; but he refused to give me any information upon the subject, saying he was not at liberty to do so. All he would say of the matter was that his mother had requested him to give me the note, and await my reading of it. For a few moments I felt undecided as to going to the house of Mrs. Leighton; but, the thought that she was ill, and had sent for me, caused me to come to the decision that I would grant her request. I feared not to meet Mrs. Leighton, for I had done her no wrong. I therefore told Lewis that in a few moments I would be ready to accompany him. My uncle wished to send the carriage with me; but I told him it was quite unnecessary, as the distance was short and the evening was very fine, and Lewis had said he would accompany me when I wished to return home.

A few minutes' walk brought me to the dwelling of Mrs. Leighton. Lewis conducted me at once to his mother's apartment. I saw as yet no other member of the family. After ushering me into the room, he withdrew, and left me alone with Mrs. Leighton. I quietly advanced into the room and paused before her. She was reclining in a large easy chair, and I was much surprised by her changed appearance. She was very thin and pale, and appeared to be weak and languid; and Mrs. Harringford's letter was recalled to my mind when I observed how gray was her once beautiful hair. She extended her hand to me; but, for some moments, was unable to utter a word. When she relinquished the hand I had given her, she motioned me to a seat. She seemed agitated by some painful emotion. I was the first to break the silence, which I did by saying,—

"Whatever may have been your object, Mrs. Leighton, in seeking this interview, you will see, by the readiness with which I have responded to your request, that I cherish no resentment toward you."

Becoming more composed, she replied to me in a low voice, saying,—

"As I was unable to go to you, I sent for you, that I may humbly ask your forgiveness for the injustice you have suffered from me. I now acknowledge, what you are probably already aware of, that it was a foolish and false pride which influenced my conduct toward you, when you left my house long ago. It requires reverses of fortune to convince us of the vanity of all earthly things; and reverses have overtaken me. And, more than this, my failing health admonishes me that, unless a change for the better soon takes place, my days on earth will soon be numbered. During all the time that has passed since we have met, my mind has never been at rest; for, though too proud to acknowledge it, I have ever been sensible that I treated you with cruelty and injustice. But my pride is now humbled, and I beg of you to forgive me; for, believe me, I have suffered even more than you."

I extended my hand to her, saying,—

"I freely and fully forgive all the past, Mrs. Leighton, and I trust we may be friends for the future."

After sitting silent for a few moments, Mrs. Leighton again addressed me, saying,—

"Were it in your power, Clara, would you make me entirely happy?"

I replied that certainly I would. She regarded me earnestly as she said,—

"Will you become Willie's wife?"

I knew not what reply to make to a question so unexpected. At length I said,—

"Willie has been a long time absent. He may have changed his mind; or, he may be already married."

"I will answer for all that," replied Mrs. Leighton. "Willie is here. He arrived two days since, and would have called to see you ere this, but I begged him to defer calling till I had seen you, and acknowledged my former injustice to you; for I now am sensible that I wronged a worthy and noble girl."

Remember, kind reader, that, although I had expected never again to meet with Willie Leighton, I still loved him with all the strength of a first love.

Before I could frame a reply to the last remark of Mrs. Leighton, the door opened, and Willie, accompanied by his father, entered the room.

I pass over our meeting. But Mr. Leighton, soon after, placing my hand in that of Willie, said,—

"God bless you, my children; may you be happy."

When I returned home that evening, it was Willie, not Lewis, who accompanied me.

CHAPTER XXII.

CLARA'S MARRIAGE.

WILLIE was anxious that an early day should be appointed for our marriage; but I was unwilling that our marriage should take place until the ensuing spring. I wished not so suddenly to leave my uncle for the long wedding tour which Willie had in contemplation.

Laura and Georgania, accompanied by their husbands, came at Christmas to visit their parents. It was indeed a joyful family reunion. We accepted our present happiness, and made no unpleasant allusions to the past. If Georgania retained any of her old ways that were not agreeable, I was too much occupied by my own new-found happiness to be annoyed by them.

Willie generously urged his father to use a portion of the wealth he had inherited from his deceased relative in settling his deranged business affairs, and Mr. Leighton finally accepted the noble offer. Accordingly, he paid off the debts, and again started a business, which, if on a smaller scale than formerly, rested on a firmer basis.

During the winter, my uncle made a will, bestowing the chief part of his wealth upon me. The house in which we resided, he intended as a wedding-gift, saying that we must accept of the gift encumbered by the giver, as he wished to reside with me during the remainder of his life.

"I have reserved enough," said my uncle, "for my own private use; and who has so rightful a claim to the wealth which a kind Providence has bestowed upon me, as the daughter of my twin-brother?"

From the time of Willie's return, the health of Mrs. Leighton slowly, but surely, improved; and, when winter softened into the balmy days of spring, her health became fully restored.

We were married on the twentieth of May; and, as Willie had decided upon England for our wedding tour, we sailed immediately after our marriage. We returned to our home, in Philadelphia, in October.

We soon found ourselves permanently settled in our own home, to the great joy of Mrs. O'Flaherty, who still retained her position as house-keeper.

"Indade, me daar misthress," said she, "an' it's good to see yees at home agin; for wasn't this the lonesome place whiles ye was absint."

Soon after our return, I mentioned the promise which I made long ago to Aunt Patience, that if I ever should possess a home of my own, I would receive her as an inmate of that home.

"I well remember," replied Willie, "the kind aunt who attended your mother during her last illness, and I will gladly do my utmost to render happy her declining years."

I had secretly felt some fears that my uncle might object to our receiving Aunt Patience to our home. A short time after, I mentioned the matter to my uncle, telling him of my mother's dying injunction to me, that I should not neglect Aunt Patience in her old age. His reply put all my fears to flight.

"I am glad, Clara," said my uncle, "to see that you respect the wishes of your deceased mother. Our dwelling is large, and we can surely find room for Aunt Patience. I will go for her myself, as I am at leisure, and would enjoy the journey."

With a light heart, I wrote to Aunt Patience, informing her of our intentions; and, a few days later, my uncle set out on his journey to Massachusetts. When he returned, accompanied by my aged relative, tears mingled with my welcome, so vividly was my mother recalled to my mind by the meeting.

CHAPTER XXIII.

A PLEASING INCIDENT.

AGAIN it is the twentieth of May; and, this day five years ago, was my wedding-day. Two years since, and the fountain of a new love was stirred in my heart, namely, the love of a mother for her first-born son. One year since, I was called to stand by the dying-bed of Aunt Patience. Her end was peace; and her earthly remains rest beside those of my mother.

My uncle still lives with us, a hale and vigorous old man, over seventy years of age. The parents of Willie still reside in the city. Birdie and Lewis are both at home. Lewis assists his father in their business, which has again become very prosperous.

I bring my story to a close by relating an incident which took place the summer succeeding the date of this chapter. I had long wished to visit my friends in New Hampshire; but my own cares had hitherto prevented me; but this season I decided to pay the long-deferred visit. Willie was very glad to accompany me, having long wished to visit the Eastern States. Birdie and Lewis also bore us company.

As our way lay through a portion of Massachusetts, I determined once more to visit the small village which formerly had been the home of Aunt Patience. We arrived at Woodville late on a Saturday evening, and on Sabbath morning were invited to hear a talented young preacher, who, we were informed, had lately been called as pastor to the Congregational Church in that village. As the young minister ascended the pulpit, his countenance struck me as being strangely familiar. As I was endeavoring to decide in my own mind where I could have before met him, it suddenly occurred to me that the young preacher was no other than my old friend, Obadiah Hawkins; and when, upon again raising my eyes, I encountered one of those old-time furtive glances, I felt certain that I was right in my conjecture. The rough-looking youth, whom I had once thought so uncomely, had changed to a really fine looking man. When the services were closed, I at once made my way to him; and, as he had already recognized me, we soon renewed our former acquaintance. I introduced him to Willie, also to Birdie and Lewis. During the few days we remained at Woodville, the young preacher called frequently. He soon evinced a marked partiality for the society of Birdie, and, strange as it may seem, I observed that she was deeply interested in him. I know not how the matter may end, but I do know that, since our return home, Birdie receives frequent letters, addressed in a gentleman's hand, and post-marked "Woodville." Who knows but Obadiah Hawkins may yet be my brother-in-law?

In taking a retrospective view of the past, and contrasting it with the happy present, I feel that the consoling words which, in a dream, my mother uttered to me, years ago, have been more than verified,—"Fear not, my beloved daughter; only continue in the path of duty, and all will yet be well."

THE END.